*She was acutely aware that Cable Montana was, indeed, husband material.*

He could have it all if he so desired, could pick his life's partner from the vast selection of available women in town. He could ste ⬚⬚⬚⬚ ⬚at encompassed ⬚⬚⬚⬚⬚⬚⬚⬚⬚⬚⬚⬚⬚⬚⬚⬚⬚ overflow with ⬚⬚⬚⬚⬚⬚⬚⬚⬚⬚⬚⬚⬚na did not have to go ⬚⬚⬚⬚⬚⬚⬚⬚⬚⬚⬚hoose to do so.

But Lindsey Pa⬚⬚⬚⬚⬚⬚⬚⬚⬚le was out of reach. What he ⬚⬚presented was beyond what she could ever call her own. She would never marry anyone. Never.

Her little secret would see to that....

Dear Reader,

**What if…?** These two little words serve as the springboard for each romance novel that bestselling author Joan Elliott Pickart writes. "I always go back to that age-old question. My ideas come straight from imagination," she says. And with more than thirty Silhouette novels to her credit, the depth of Joan's imagination seems bottomless! Joan started by taking a class to learn how to write a romance and "felt that this was where I belonged," she recalls. This month Joan delivers *Her Little Secret,* the next from THE BABY BET, where you'll discover what if…a sheriff and a lovely nursery owner decide to foil town matchmakers and "act" like lovers.…

And don't miss the other compelling "what ifs" in this month's Silhouette Special Edition lineup. What if a U.S. Marshal knee-deep in his father's murder investigation discovers his former love is expecting his child? Read *Seven Months and Counting…* by Myrna Temte, the next installment in the STOCKWELLS OF TEXAS series. What if an army ranger, who believes dangerous missions are no place for a woman, learns the only person who can help rescue his sister is a female? Lindsay McKenna brings you this exciting story in *Man with a Mission,* the next book in her MORGAN'S MERCENARIES: MAVERICK HEARTS series. What happens if a dutiful daughter falls in love with the one man her family forbids? Look for Christine Flynn's *Forbidden Love.* What if a single dad falls for a pampered beauty who is not at all accustomed to small-town happily-ever-after? Find out in Nora Roberts's *Considering Kate,* the next in THE STANISLASKIS. And what if the girl-next-door transforms herself to get a man's attention—but is noticed by someone else? Make sure to pick up Barbara McMahon's *Starting with a Kiss.*

**What if…** Two words with endless possibilities. If you've got your own "what if" scenario, start writing. Silhouette Special Edition would love to read about it.

Happy reading!

Karen Taylor Richman,
Senior Editor

Please address questions and book requests to:
Silhouette Reader Service
U.S.: 3010 Walden Ave., P.O. Box 1325, Buffalo, NY 14269
Canadian: P.O. Box 609, Fort Erie, Ont. L2A 5X3

# Her Little Secret

## JOAN ELLIOTT PICKART

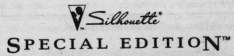

# SPECIAL EDITION™

Published by Silhouette Books

**America's Publisher of Contemporary Romance**

For Autumn,
who was waiting for me
to bring her home.
*I love you, Bug.*

 SILHOUETTE BOOKS

ISBN 0-373-24377-4

HER LITTLE SECRET

Visit Silhouette at www.eHarlequin.com

**Printed in U.S.A.**

## JOAN ELLIOTT PICKART

is the author of over seventy novels. When she isn't writing, she enjoys watching football, knitting, reading, gardening and attending craft shows on the town square. Joan has three all-grown-up daughters and a fantastic little grandson. In September of 1995, Joan traveled to China to adopt her fourth daughter, Autumn. Joan and Autumn have settled into their cozy cottage in a charming, small town in the high pine country of Arizona.

# THE MacALLISTER FAMILY TREE

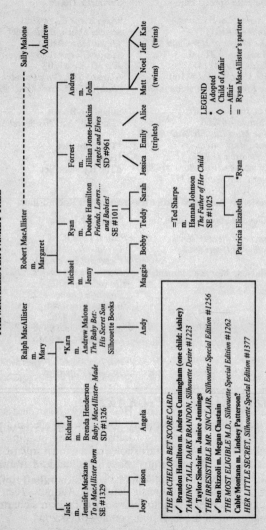

Sally Malone
◇Andrew

Robert MacAllister
m.
Margaret

Ralph MacAllister
m.
Mary

Michael
m.
Jenny

Ryan
m.
Deedee Hamilton
*Friends, Lovers…
and Babies!*
SE #1011

Forrest
m.
Jillian Jones-Jenkins
*Angels and Elves*
SD #961

Andrea
m.
John

*Kara
m.
Andrew Malone
*The Baby Bet:
His Secret Son*
Silhouette Books

Richard
m.
Brenda Henderson
*Baby: MacAllister-Made*
SD #1326

Jack
m.
Jennifer Mackane
*To a MacAllister Born*
SE #1329

Andy

Angela

Joey    Jason

Maggie   Bobby   Teddy   Sarah   Jessica   Emily   Alice
                                              (triplets)

Matt   Noel   Jeff   Kate
   (twins)        (twins)

=Ted Sharpe

Hannah Johnson
*The Father of Her Child*
SE #1025

Patricia Elizabeth        *Ryan

### LEGEND
- Adopted
◇ Child of Affair
--- Affair
= Ryan MacAllister's partner

*THE BACHELOR BET SCORE CARD:*
✓ Brandon Hamilton m. Andrea Cunningham (one child: Ashley)
*TAMING TALL, DARK BRANDON, Silhouette Desire #1223*
✓ Taylor Sinclair m. Janice Jennings
*THE IRRESISTIBLE MR. SINCLAIR, Silhouette Special Edition #1256*
✓ Ben Rizzoli m. Megan Chastain
*THE MOST ELIGIBLE M.D., Silhouette Special Edition #1262*
Cable Montana m. Lindsey Patterson?
*HER LITTLE SECRET, Silhouette Special Edition #1377*

## Chapter One

Cable Montana drove slowly along the deserted road, nodding in appreciation of the picture-perfect June day. The windows on his Land Rover were open, allowing a cool breeze to float through the vehicle, offering the aromas of wildflowers and pine trees.

He remembered that Ben Rizzoli had once said that every season in Prescott was his favorite when it arrived and that living in the mile-high small town sure beat being part of the heat and hubbub of frantic Phoenix, which was a hundred miles down the mountain.

After being in Prescott, Arizona, for a year and a half, he thoroughly agreed with his buddy, Ben. Prescott was as close to perfection as it could get, and won hands down over the existence he'd had in Nevada, too.

Yep, he was here to stay. Providing, of course, that the good folks elected him sheriff in a couple of years when his appointed-by-the-mayor term ended. He'd stepped in when the previous sheriff had suddenly decided to retire, but next time around he'd have to win an election to keep his position.

According to the grapevine, though—and heaven knows that Prescott's gossip mill was always thriving—there was little chance of anyone running against him in the next election. He'd been warmly welcomed to the town, not only as the sheriff but as a citizen.

Life, Cable thought, making no attempt to curb his smile, was good. He had some fantastic friends here, enjoyed his job, was comfortable in the small, cozy house he was renting and, in about another fifteen minutes, he was going to pick up his new German shepherd puppy and take him home.

"Gotta think of a name for the little guy," Cable said aloud. "We're going to be a great team…a man and his dog, just like in the old western flicks."

Of course, in the movies there was always a pretty schoolteacher for the sheriff to woo and win. Not so for Sheriff Cable Montana, which was exactly the way he wanted it.

He'd done the love, marriage, then divorce nightmare and had no intention of traveling down that road again. No way.

He hadn't even dated since arriving in Prescott, which had proven to be a wise decision. Ben had hinted more than once that a bevy of matchmakers would be lurking in the shadows waiting to pounce on the new sheriff. By staying completely out of the social scene he'd kept the matchmakers at bay.

Cable frowned.

Or had he?

Now that he thought about it, in the past couple of months since the summer residents had returned to town from their winter homes in warmer climates, there had been a sudden rush of invitations to dinner at homes where a single woman was among the guests for the evening.

Elderly ladies had stopped by his house and the office with baked goods, saying that Miss So-and-so had made this, but it was more than they could possibly eat so why didn't he enjoy it, too. And wasn't Miss Whoever just a marvel in the kitchen?

There had been three calls to the office on nights when he'd been on duty in which the callers said they were sure they'd seen a prowler at Miss Somebody's house, and would Sheriff Montana go right over there and check it out?

"Oh, hell," Cable said, his eyes widening.

Where had his brain been? He'd gotten complacent, had decided months before that the matchmakers weren't going to zero in on him, despite Ben's warnings. They'd labeled him a hopeless case, he'd figured, because he hadn't even taken a woman out to dinner since arriving in town.

But he now had a sneaking feeling that the elderly ladies in question were in the process of leaping into action.

What did they do? Give a guy a year or so to settle in, watch his progress—or lack of same—in the social arena, and if he didn't pass muster, they rallied the troops and attacked?

Oh, man, what a depressing thought. He didn't need this hassle. Sure, he would have enjoyed a woman's company during the past months, would have liked some female companionship for dinner and a movie. But that was a luxury he couldn't afford in a town where matchmaking, so said Ben Rizzoli, was one of the favorite pastimes of the older-ladies set.

Well, one thing was for damn sure. He'd better come out of the ether and pay attention, because it appeared that he just might be the next unfortunate soul chosen to be the target of the everyone-should-fall-in-love-and-get-married contingent.

Cable's gloomy thoughts were blessedly halted as he saw the turnoff he was watching for. He drove slowly along a bumpy dirt road, then parked in front of a well-kept house that had several large chain-link enclosures in the rear area.

As he walked toward the pens, an attractive woman in her mid-fifties waved and started toward him, meeting him by one of the pens. His arrival had caused a multitude of dogs to start barking and he had to raise his voice to be heard above the din.

"Hello, Gwen," Cable said, smiling.

"Good to see you, Sheriff," Gwen said, matching his smile. "You're right on time and your baby is ready to go. He's had a bath and is spit-shined and pretty. What are you going to name him?"

"I don't know yet," Cable said. "He's going to be my buddy and I have to give him a name that will…hey, that's it. I'll call him Buddy."

Gwen laughed. "That was easy enough." She paused. "Say, did I tell you that my daughter is coming back to Prescott to live? Her divorce is final and she's going to move in with me and help me run this place.

"There's a lot of work to breeding dogs and it's getting to be a bit much for me to handle since my husband passed on. Betty Lou, my daughter, is a fine girl, just lovely. She simply made a mistake when she picked that man she married. She's got four kids, darling children, well-mannered and so adorable.

"I just thought I'd mention that Betty Lou will be here in a couple of weeks. You might want to meet her, what with you two being about the same age and all…and you both love dogs. Know what I mean?"

Oh, yeah, Cable thought, mentally rolling his eyes heavenward, he knew what she meant, all right. And ding, there was his matchmaking alarm going off in his head.

"Boy," Cable said, then glanced at his watch, "look at the time. I'd better collect Buddy and get moving here. Do I owe you any more on my account?"

"Nope, you're paid in full," Gwen said. "I'll go get your boy. You will think about meeting Betty Lou, won't you, Sheriff?"

"You bet," he said. He'd think about it for five seconds maximum and draw the "not-in-this-lifetime" conclusion. "Buddy?"

"Right."

As Gwen turned and hurried away, Cable shook his head and sighed.

"Montana," he said under his breath, "you're in deep, deep trouble."

* * *

Early the next morning, an exhausted Cable arrived at the sheriff's office with Buddy peering over the side of a box, his front paws perched on the edge.

It hadn't taken long for Cable to discover that he was the proud papa of an eight-week-old furry bundle of energy. Buddy had run around Cable's fenced backyard with such enthusiasm that he tumbled over his own feet more often than not, then scrambled up and started off again.

Buddy liked his Puppy Chow dinner, which he had consumed in a frenzy, his chew toy that squeaked and was shaped like a pork chop, and tearing the newspaper that Cable had attempted to read with Buddy perched on his lap.

What Buddy Montana did *not* like was being all alone in the box with the rug on the bottom where he was supposed to sleep during the night next to Cable's bed. He'd voiced his lonely displeasure with ear-splitting wails and futile attempts to climb out of his unacceptable quarters.

At two in the morning Cable had groaned in defeat and scooped Buddy out of the box. A peaceful silence had fallen as Buddy curled up in a ball and slept the remaining hours of the night on Cable's chest.

Mary-Margaret Moore, a grandmother in her fifties who had worked as the sheriff's secretary, as well as the radio dispatcher for thirty years, fell in love at first sight of the puppy.

"Oh, look at that baby," she said, patting Buddy on the head. "Isn't he the cutest thing?"

Cable laughed. "He wasn't very cute at two this morning, but we worked it out. His name is Buddy, and I'm going to train him to behave here at the office, then ride with me on patrol. It doesn't make sense to get a dog, then leave him all alone in the yard while I'm at work."

"You're such a thoughtful daddy, Cable," Mary-Margaret said. "You should have a bunch of kids of your own to play with this little sweetheart. Of course, you'd need a wife first."

"No, thank you," Cable said. "Anything happening here that I should know about?"

"Nope. The deputies are out keeping peace among the multitudes. You have a stack of paperwork on your desk that needs your attention, though. Have you ever noticed how pretty that Kimberly Swanson is? You know, that young woman who owns the yogurt shop downtown?"

Cable frowned. "I don't like yogurt."

"That's beside the point," Mary-Margaret said. "The fact remains that Kimberly is an attractive *single* woman, who has a smile for everyone.

"She was dating Tucker Jones for a spell. You

know, the plumber? Anyway, that didn't seem to work out, so Kimberly is available. As the sheriff, it's your civic duty to get to know all the business-people in town, Cable. You ought to stop by the yogurt shop and say howdy to Kimberly.''

Cable narrowed his eyes. ''Why are you suggesting this after all this time?''

''Well, Kimberly was tied up with Tucker for some months, so there was no sense in bringing up the subject,'' Mary-Margaret said, shrugging. ''Besides, don't you think you're overdue to start dating?''

''Not really,'' he said, shifting the box and Buddy higher onto his chest. ''Tell me something, Mary-Margaret. Has there been a campaign launched by the matchmakers of Prescott to see to it that I get married?''

''My stars, what a fanciful idea, Cable,'' Mary-Margaret said, batting her eyelashes at him. ''You're a grown man who is certainly capable of managing his own social life. Not that you're doing a ripsnorting job of it, mind you, but do you honestly believe that a group of women have sat around together discussing you in such a fashion?''

Cable nodded slowly. ''It has crossed my mind, Mary-Margaret.''

''Don't you think we have better things to do,

Sheriff Montana?'' Mary-Margaret said with an indignant little sniff.

''No.''

''Oh. Have you given any thought to potty training?'' Mary-Margaret said.

''Huh?'' Cable said, his eyes widening.

''Buddy just tinkled in the box,'' Mary-Margaret said, smiling sweetly.

''Hell,'' Cable said, then strode toward his office.


Just before lunch, Cable glanced up from the report he was reading to see a rather plump, smiling woman in her thirties standing in the doorway of his office.

He got to his feet, searching his mind for the woman's name. She looked vaguely familiar, but his mental file came up empty.

''May I help you?'' he said.

''I'm Valerie Adams?'' the woman said, walking to the front of Cable's desk. ''We met at the bazaar at the Episcopal church? Just before Christmas last year? I was tending the booth with the homemade popcorn balls that had been colored green and red for the holidays?''

Cable nodded, then told himself to keep his head still, having realized that he'd been raising his chin at the end of each of Valerie's statements presented as a question.

"Oh, yes, the popcorn balls," he said. "What can I do for you Mrs. Adams?"

"It's *Ms.* Adams, Sheriff," she said, smiling. "I just heard that you have a new puppy? Named Buddy?" She glanced at the floor where Buddy was happily shredding a piece of newspaper. "I have a poodle puppy? Her name is Paris? I was wondering if you'd like to arrange a play date for Paris and Buddy? I could cook us some supper and the little ones could get to know each other?"

"I…um…Buddy is a bit young for…for play dates," Cable said. "I appreciate the offer, but I'm afraid I'll have to pass. Thanks for coming by, Ms. Adams. Perhaps I'll see you at the next bazaar? At Christmastime? At the church?"

Cripes, he thought. Now he was talking like this woman, his voice rising at the end of each sentence he was stumbling around to produce.

"Well, I…fine," Valerie said with a huff, then spun around and headed toward the doorway. "I'll save you a popcorn ball."

"Appreciate it," Cable said, then sank back onto his old, creaking leather chair.

He leaned his head on the high back of the chair and stared at the ceiling.

"I'm not going to survive this," he said aloud.

"They're out to get me, Buddy, no doubt about it."

Buddy bounced across the room, wiggled under the desk on his tummy and began to chew on the toe of one of Cable's western boots.

During the next two weeks, Cable's nerves were stretched to the limit. On three occasions, gushing young women appeared on his front porch with covered dishes in hand, all declaring that anyone with a "new baby" in the house shouldn't have to worry about what to prepare for dinner. Cable had mumbled his thank-yous, but had definitely not invited any of the gift givers to enter the house.

To make matters worse, all three of the meals had been tuna-fish casseroles, which he detested. How he was going to return the dishes to the women was a problem he refused to address. He placed the clean, empty containers on a high shelf in his pantry and closed the door each time with a decisive thump.

He politely refused four invitations to homes for dinner, declaring that he was buried in paperwork that was taking up his leisure hours.

He was under a full-blown matchmaking attack, Cable realized miserably, and it was driving him nuts. Everyone suddenly seemed to have a single daughter, granddaughter, niece, cousin, and on the

list went, that they just knew the sheriff would be
delighted to meet.

To his own self-disgust, Cable began to peek
around the edge of the curtains on the front window of his house before automatically answering
a knock on his door. More often than not, he stood
statue still, hardly breathing, until the woman on
his porch gave up and left, leaving her offering of
food on the mat.

Cable added empty plates, tins and pans, which
had contained a variety of baked goods, to the
growing number of containers in his pantry.

While walking through town on foot patrol, he
began to feel edgy, glancing often over his shoulder to see if he was about to be descended upon
by a member of the female populace of Prescott.

For the sake of his diminishing sanity he told
Mary-Margaret and the night-shift radio dispatcher
to send a deputy on any calls coming in that involved a single woman, a demand that earned him
a narrow-eyed glare from Mary-Margaret.

When Cable had had Buddy for a little more
than two weeks, he returned from a trip to the grocery store, where the checkout woman had smiled
at him coyly, to discover that Buddy had dug up
a small lilac bush in the backyard. Buddy was
growling, wagging his tail and dragging the bush

around the yard when Cable stepped outside the kitchen door.

"Oh, cripes," he said, striding toward the puppy. "No, Buddy, cut it out. That's not a toy. It's not yours. It's…damn."

He rescued the bush and held it at arm's length as Buddy spun in a tight circle, yipping with obvious pride at his accomplishment. The puppy finally flopped over in a dizzy, furry heap, his little tongue hanging out the side of his mouth.

"You tore off the roots on this poor thing," Cable said, frowning. "I'm arresting you for assault on a lilac bush, Buddy."

Buddy rolled over onto his back and thumped his tail on the grass.

"You're a rotten little guy," Cable said. "I have to replace this, you know, before the landlord sees what you've done." He tossed the bush on the ground and scooped up the puppy, holding him at eye level. "You're dangerous, you know that? You're coming to the nursery with me to buy a new bush, which you better not touch once it's planted. How am I going to keep you from digging up everything there is in this yard?"

Buddy licked Cable on the nose.

Fifteen minutes later, Cable was wandering around the outside display area of The Green

Thumb nursery while Buddy tugged on the leash his master held. Buddy was sniffing and snorting as he discovered one new aroma after another.

Cable started down another row of plants, then stopped, a frown knitting his brows as he heard an attractive young woman talking to a grandmotherly woman.

"This is a Christmas cactus, Mildred," the younger woman said. "Does this resemble the picture you saw in the magazine? From the way you described it, I think this is what you're looking for."

"Oh, yes, Lindsey, that's it," the older woman said, beaming. "The picture was an ad for carpet cleaner, so I didn't have a clue as to what the pretty plant was that they showed having been spilled on the floor. I only knew that I wanted one, then couldn't remember where I put the magazine with the picture of it. You're such a dear."

"Well, I'm glad I had this in stock," Lindsey said, smiling.

"Your own home must be gorgeous," Mildred said, "since you know so much about plants and all. I mean, heavenly days, you have your own nursery."

Lindsey laughed and Cable jerked slightly as the happy sound caused an unexpected and unwelcomed frisson of heat to slither down his spine.

"You know how it goes," Lindsey said. "The cobbler's children have no shoes. I really don't have that many plants at home."

"Nor do you have children," Mildred said, adding a *tsk* to the statement. "Or a husband. A pretty young woman like you should be married and bouncing a baby on your hip, Lindsey."

"This plant nursery keeps me very busy," Lindsey said, "with no time left for a baby nursery at home."

"There's always time for romance in a person's life," Mildred said.

Uh-oh, Cable thought. He was out of there. Lindsey Whoever was apparently single and that was causing him to go on red-alert. There was another nursery across town that he could go to.

He was not about to have a one-on-one conversation with an eligible female. He didn't care what she'd said about her business keeping her too busy for a husband and kids. Single was single, and single was dangerous.

As Cable began to turn, tugging on Buddy's leash, the older woman spotted him.

"Sheriff Montana," she called. "Isn't this a nice surprise?"

Oh, hell, Cable thought, producing a small smile as he turned back around.

"Come, come," Mildred said, "and say hello to

Lindsey. Or have you two met already? Is this a social call you're making, Sheriff?''

Cable walked slowly forward with Buddy leading the way, tail wagging to beat the band.

"No, this is an emergency trip," Cable said, stopping in front of the two women and looking at the older one. "Buddy dug up a lilac bush in the backyard and I need to replace it. I'm just making a quick stop here. Very quick."

"Then you don't know our Lindsey?" Mildred said, raising her eyebrows.

"No, but—"

"Well, I'll take care of that right now. Lindsey Patterson, this is our sheriff Cable Montana and his sweet puppy Buddy. Sheriff, this is Lindsey Patterson, owner of The Green Thumb. There. Now you two have been officially introduced."

Cable shifted his gaze slowly and very reluctantly to Lindsey, then felt as though he'd been punched in the gut when their eyes met.

Whoa, he thought, taking a short, sharp breath. This was one beautiful woman standing in front of him. She was tall, slender, and her jeans and T-shirt outlined her figure nicely, very nicely.

Her hair was short, blond and curly, her features delicate, her skin lightly tanned, and she had the biggest brown eyes he'd ever seen. Eyes, he realized, that were dancing with merriment.

"Sheriff," Lindsey said, dipping her head slightly. "It's a pleasure to meet you."

So, this was Sheriff Montana, Lindsey thought. Despite the fact that he'd been in town for over a year, she'd never seen him anywhere, but she'd definitely heard about the heartthrob of Prescott. The women were in a tizzy over the hunky new lawman.

And with just cause, she admitted. He was ruggedly handsome, over six feet tall, with wide shoulders and long, powerful legs. His hair was black as night and needed a trim. And those eyes. Good grief, she'd never seen such green eyes. Did the good sheriff wear colored contact lenses to further dazzle the ladies?

"Ms. Patterson," Cable said, touching the brim of his Stetson with his index finger.

"Oh, I just had a marvelous idea," Mildred said, as she clutched the pot holding the Christmas cactus. "There's going to be a box supper at the Methodist church next Sunday after services. Why don't you two join us and—"

"I'm busy," Cable said.

"I have too much work to do," Lindsey said, at exactly the same time.

Mildred frowned. "You young people must learn that there is more to life than furthering your careers and your monetary worth."

"Yes, ma'am," Cable said.

"I'll certainly give that some thought," Lindsey said, unable to curb her smile.

"Sheriff," Mildred went on, "did you enjoy the coconut fig cookies my second cousin's granddaughter baked for you? She said you weren't home when she dropped by, so she left them at your door. You haven't been home much lately, from what I hear."

"The cookies were very nice," Cable said. "Coconut and figs. Can't beat that combination. No, ma'am, you sure can't."

Lindsey camouflaged a burst of laughter with a faked cough that earned her a glare from Cable.

"I remember those coconut fig cookies," Lindsey said. "I do believe that was the kind that Barney Barrister whipped up and brought by here a year or so ago for me to sample. The recipe certainly does get around."

"Yes, well, Barney has a wife to bake cookies for him now," Mildred said. "He was married in the spring to that lovely little...well, she isn't exactly little at over two hundred pounds...but she has a sweet smile."

"I heard that Barney got married," Lindsey said, nodding. "I must drop by and return that cookie plate he left here. I'm sure his wife could use it in the kitchen when she bakes those yummy coconut fig cookies for good ol' Barn.''

"They're a darling couple," Mildred said. "Well, I must be off. Thank you again, Lindsey, for helping me find the plant from the carpet ad. I'm just delighted with my Christmas cactus. I'll go on inside and pay for this at the register where your assistant is. You tend to the sheriff's needs, dear."

"Thank you for coming by," Lindsey said. "Have a nice day, Mildred."

"You, too, Lindsey," Mildred said. "Goodbye, Sheriff Montana. Oh, and by the way, your puppy just fell asleep on your foot. Ta-ta, children."

Cable looked down and saw that Buddy was, indeed, sleeping with his head on the toe of one of Cable's boots, and mentally expressed his gratitude to the dog for being in need of a nap.

This was the perfect excuse to leave, before the not-married Ms. Patterson had a chance to pounce. He'd simply act like an eccentric who believed a puppy should sleep in its own bed for the sake of its psyche.

"Well, Buddy is down for the count," Cable said, still staring at the dog. "I'd better get him home where he belongs so he doesn't become disoriented when he wakens, poor little guy."

Cable snapped his head up as he heard Lindsey

burst into laughter. She laughed until she had to wipe tears from her cheeks, then wrapped her arms around her stomach. Cable frowned and ignored the coil of heat that had been ignited low in his body at the delightful sound.

"Do you have a problem, Ms. Patterson?" he said finally.

"Oh, my," she said, taking a much-needed breath. "What a hoot. The ever-famous coconut fig cookies. Tell me, Sheriff Montana, do you like tuna-fish casserole?"

Ding went the alarm in Cable's head.

"No, ma'am, I don't," he said, tugging his Stetson lower on his forehead. "I appreciate the offer you're making, but I'll have to pass on tuna-fish—"

"Halt," Lindsey interrupted, raising one hand. "I'm not offering to make you a tuna-fish casserole. I'm just wondering if you were enjoying the ones that are being delivered to your door. I hate that stuff. Especially the ones that have the peas in them.

"Now there's a meal for you. Tuna-fish casserole with peas, and coconut fig cookies for dessert. Oh, how gross. My sympathies, Sheriff. I have walked in your shoes. I hope you realize that your sanity is at stake." She burst into laughter again.

"You've lost me here," Cable said.

"I was the target of the matchmakers of Prescott

a year or so ago,'' Lindsey said, smiling, ''and lived to tell about it. They finally gave up on me. Thank goodness.''

''Oh, I see,'' Cable said, nodding. ''How long do they keep this up?''

''Months. Months and months and months,'' Lindsey said merrily. ''I still haven't returned all the covered dishes I have stashed away at home. I don't believe for one minute that all the men who brought me those god-awful things actually prepared them. It's a conspiracy, no doubt about it, and your ticket has been punched.''

''I know,'' Cable said, then sighed.

''Well, good luck and happy eating.'' Lindsey paused. ''Did you say you need to replace a lilac bush that your Buddy dug up?''

''Yes, but…yes.''

''Okay, but what's to keep him from digging up the new one?'' Lindsey said, frowning. ''Are there other bushes and plants in your yard?''

''A whole slew of them,'' Cable said. ''Buddy isn't home alone all that much because I take him to work with me, but I sure can't have him destroying the yard when I do leave him out there. I'm only renting the place and I'll have to repair any damage he does.''

''There are several types of enclosure material available to protect your landscaping,'' Lindsey said. ''I can't really recommend the best for your situation unless I actually see what is growing in your yard. I could come over, plant the new bush, then recommend what I believe would be the answer to the problem.''

Ding, Cable thought. Lindsey Patterson was very tricky. She had attempted to give the impression that she had no desire to find a husband, but now? Son of a gun if she wasn't offering to drop by his place. She must think he was a gullible dope. Well, he had news for the sneaky Ms. Patterson.

''Well,'' he said, ''I don't think it's necessary for you to—''

''I'd need to know your work schedule,'' Lindsey went on, ''so I could come by when you and Buddy weren't home.''

''Pardon me?''

''If you'd like to hire me to do this, it would be best if Buddy didn't see me planting the new bush, or installing whatever I decide to use to protect everything. I don't want him digging a hole just because I am.''

''Oh.''

''Yes, that's the best plan,'' Lindsey said. ''I'll take care of things at your house when you're away. I can mail you a bill, if you like.'' She shrugged. ''The fact of the matter is, you'll probably never see me again.''

## Chapter Two

Lindsey Patterson had just sent him packing…big time, Cable thought incredulously, as he drove away from The Green Thumb.

And his ridiculous reaction to Ms. Patterson's very smooth brush-off? Instead of being grateful that at least one single woman in this town wasn't setting her matrimonial sights on him, he was very aware of a borderline-disgusting sense of having suffered a blow to his male ego.

But, gripe, the woman had made it crystal clear that she intended to conduct her plant-nursery chores in his backyard when he wasn't home, thank you very much, and had tacked on that they would probably never see each other again. *Oh, well, who cares,* was the attitude of the lovely Ms. Patterson.

And she really was lovely, Cable mused. There was a fresh, wholesome aura about Lindsey. The jeans she'd been wearing didn't have a designer label on the back pocket—so, okay, he had admittedly slid a glance at her nicely rounded bottom. Nor did it appear that she wore any makeup on her pretty face. She had no uppity qualms about getting her delicate hands dirty, as evidenced by the career she'd chosen.

Her laughter was like wind chimes on a breezy summer day, and those eyes...those great big, beautiful brown eyes were enough to turn a man inside out. Then there were her lips, those kissable lips that had created smiles that had knocked his socks off.

Oh, yes, Lindsey was definitely a very delectable woman, but he had obviously held about as much appeal to her as a root canal. Nothing quite like this had ever happened to him before, that was for damn sure.

"Montana," he said aloud, "you're nuts. Count your blessings, idiot. There won't be a tuna-fish casserole delivered to your door, with or without peas, by Lindsey Patterson."

Lindsey certainly had laughed herself silly over his predicament with the matchmakers of Prescott. She was a veteran of that war from what she'd said, and had won, been declared a hopeless case and was now left alone.

Interesting. Lindsey was pretty, *very* pretty, obviously intelligent or she wouldn't be able to make a success of her business, had a sense of humor and seemed to like puppies.

Yep, she might consider kissing his dog, but he had a dejected feeling that she would rather shoot the sheriff with his own gun before she would kiss *him.*

Why? Lindsey Patterson had everything going for her, could probably pick and choose among the bachelors in town, but she apparently had no desire to have a husband, kids, hearth and home.

What did she have against marriage? Against even dating someone, being involved in a serious relationship?

Very, *very* interesting. Intriguing. Mystifying. Fascinating and—

"Jeez, enough," Cable said, shaking his head.

He had more women dogging his heels than he even cared to think about, and here he was dwelling on the one who would probably cross the street when she saw him coming to avoid giving him the time of day.

This was so textbook-classic typical male it was nauseating. It was the old lure of the untouchable. Machismo at its worst, and he couldn't believe he'd fallen prey to it like some muscle-bound dud.

"I'm setting a terrible example for you, Buddy," Cable said, glancing over at the puppy where he was curled into a ball on the passenger seat. "Listen up, pal. If a woman isn't interested in you from the get-go, move on, don't give her another thought. Got that?"

Buddy wagged his tail.

"Good," Cable said.

Now all he had to do was figure out a way to quit thinking about the enigmatic Lindsey Patterson.

Late that night Lindsey snapped on the small lamp on the nightstand next to her bed, grabbed a book and opened it to the page marked by a slip of paper.

She read one paragraph of the mystery novel, reread it, then smacked the book closed with a sigh and tossed it next to her on the double bed.

This was ridiculous, she fumed.

She couldn't sleep.

She couldn't concentrate on the story she was in the middle of reading.

She couldn't erase the image of Cable Montana from her mind.

She was behaving like an adolescent who swooned when the quarterback of the football team spoke to her in the high school hall, or some such thing. Disgusting.

She pulled the sheet to beneath her chin, narrowed her eyes and stared at the ceiling.

So, okay, it was time for a fresh approach to this nonsense. Instead of attempting to dismiss the sheriff from her thoughts, she'd examine the situation and determine what was causing her to behave so out of character. Once she'd figured it out, she could erase Cable Montana from her memory bank.

Very good.

And yes, the light was dawning. For months now she'd been hearing about the handsome and elusive new sheriff, the hunk-of-male-stuff who had women of all ages sighing wistfully.

Despite the fact that Prescott was a small town, she simply hadn't crossed paths with the man, hadn't seen him on the streets, or in the grocery store, or at events on the town square.

Cable Montana had taken on larger-than-life proportions, due to the fact that he was the topic of endless conversations, but she hadn't seen the actual person to go with the descriptions she'd been hearing for weeks on end.

Then, lo and behold, the guy suddenly appeared before her in all his masculine splendor and she hadn't been prepared to see him and, therefore, had overreacted to being in close proximity to him.

Good gracious, had she ever overreacted, Lindsey thought, frowning. Her heart had been racing, and a strange and foreign heat had suffused her, which had been very annoying, to say the least.

The problem was, no one had exaggerated the attributes of Cable Montana. He was everything and more that the women of Prescott had been gushing about. He was drop-dead gorgeous, had a build to match, and every time she'd looked into the depths of those green eyes of his, she felt as though her bones were dissolving.

Her assistant at the nursery, Glenna-Sue, had been all atwitter over Cable being on the premises, even though Glenna-Sue was sixty-four years old, for heaven's sake.

Glenna-Sue had possessed the information that Cable's incredible green eyes were not the result of colored contact lenses, because Glenna-Sue's neighbor's brother-in-law's sister had come right out and asked the sheriff if he wore tinted contact lenses, to which he had replied in the negative.

"Big macho deal," Lindsey said with the flip of one hand. "The man has green eyes. So what?"

Green eyes fringed in long lashes that matched the midnight darkness of his hair. Green eyes that were the color of the sea. Green eyes that looked at a woman so steadily, so intently, it was as though he could see the very depths of her soul.

"Get a grip, Lindsey," she admonished herself.

Actually, her reaction was very simple. It was on the order of a child being told for months about the wondrous man named Santa Claus. Then, whamo, the kid was suddenly plunked on Santa's lap and was struck speechless at seeing the jolly old elf in living, breathing reality.

That made sense. It really did.

Of course, Sheriff Montana was as far removed from being a fat old guy in a red suit as a man could get, but that was beside the point.

She had, as embarrassing as it was to admit, succumbed to the blatant masculinity of Cable Montana like the multitudes. Her only saving grace was the knowledge that he didn't have a clue that she had been momentarily—and it had been just a flash in the pan—rattled by his presence.

If the occasion arose in the future that she was once again face-to-face with Cable, she'd be fine. Absolutely fine. She had a handle on this silliness now, understood what had happened and that was that.

Oh, thank goodness, she'd gotten this all straightened out in her head. Now, maybe, she could get some much needed sleep.

Besides, the chances of seeing Cable again were very slim. If she'd gone this many months without bumping into him, it stood to reason it would be aeons before she saw him again.

Granted, she was going to be doing some work in his backyard, but she'd set that up so she would be there when he was away from home, clever little person that she was.

"Fine." Lindsey snapped off the lamp, wiggled into a comfortable position, and closed her eyes. "I'm back to normal."

And normal was knowing that she'd never again give her heart away, fall in love. Never again.

As Lindsey drove to The Green Thumb the next morning, she was aware that a gloomy mood had settled over her, as though a dark cloud had suddenly materialized above her head to cast shadows on the sunny day.

She'd awakened at dawn to the realization that she'd dreamed about Cable Montana. She'd been so furious with herself, so unsettled, that she stomped out of the house, then had to return to retrieve the keys to her pickup truck. She'd also had to change her shoes. She'd put on one blue tennis shoe and one black one.

Darn that Sheriff Montana, she thought, reminding herself to pay attention to the traffic. Well, no, that wasn't fair. Her state of mind wasn't Cable's fault. It was what he represented that troubled her.

Cable was a very eligible bachelor, who had the potential to fall in love, get married, create a child with a special woman, be that woman's soul mate until death parted them.

Lindsey sighed.

It had been a long time since she'd been plagued with the realization that she would never again be part of a loving relationship. She would never be someone's wife, nor the mother of a child. Her existence, her world, would never include those roles.

She often went months at a stretch without dwelling on those bleak facts, had created a fragile sense of peace and contentment within herself as she devoted her energy to her thriving business.

But now? Meeting Cable Montana, knowing the focus of the matchmakers of Prescott was zeroed in on the handsome sheriff, she was acutely aware that he was, indeed, husband material.

Cable could have it all if he so desired, could pick his life's partner from the vast selection of available women in town. He could step into a world that encompassed a family, and a home that would overflow with love and laughter. Cable Montana did not have to go through life alone if he didn't choose to do so.

But Lindsey Patterson? For her, Cable was out of reach. What he represented was beyond what she could ever call her own. She would never marry anyone. Never.

Darn it, she knew that. Had known that for years now, ever since... No. She was furious at herself for the pity trip she was presently engaging in. Facts were facts. End of story. She was alone, would remain alone and was doing just fine.

Lindsey pulled into the parking lot at The Green Thumb and turned off the ignition of the truck.

And if someone looked at her crooked before she reined in her raging emotions, she thought miserably, she'd probably burst into tears.

She had to push her personal, unchangeable circumstances back into the dusty, ignored corner of her mind now...right now.

Lindsey got out of the truck and marched toward the locked gates in front of the nursery.

A nursery of plants. Not a nursery meant for babies created by exquisite lovemaking with the man who had captured her heart. Plants. She cared for them, nurtured them, even talked to them.

But none of them gave her hugs.

"Oh, Lindsey," she whispered as she unlocked the gates. "Stop it. Just stop it. Please."

To Lindsey's heartfelt relief, she was busy with customers the entire morning. Little by little her gloomy mood dissipated and by the time she ate the lunch she had packed her smiles were genuine.

In the early afternoon she left Glenna-Sue in charge of the nursery and headed for the address where Cable Montana lived and where bouncing Buddy had demolished the lilac bush.

She would plant the bush that was in the bed of the truck, then analyze the situation and decide on the best type of enclosure material to order for protecting Cable's landscaping from the busy puppy.

Lindsey parked in Cable's driveway and got out of the truck, her gaze sweeping over the small house where the sheriff lived.

Cute and cozy, she thought. This was an older section of town where some of the houses dated back to the turn of the twentieth century. Cable's house wasn't that ancient but had been there long enough to boast tall trees with leaves that whispered in the breeze.

How had he furnished it? she wondered, as she lifted the metal can containing the lilac bush from the bed of the truck. Did he have a decorating theme? Or was it done in bachelor mismatch?

Was Cable tidy, a neatnik? Or were there empty dishes in the living room, discarded clothes scattered on the floor and stacks of old newspapers and magazines by a favorite chair?

"Oh, who cares?" Lindsey said, lugging the bush as she walked toward the gate leading to the backyard.

Why was she wasting mental energy attempting to envision the interior of Cable's house? She was asking questions that she'd never know the answers to because she would have no reason to be inside Cable's home. She was being nosy, pure and simple, and enough was enough.

The afternoon summer sun beat down on her and her cheeks became flushed from the heat as she set to work. A short time later she was able to blank her mind completely as she began digging a hole larger than the one Buddy had created by pulling the lilac bush from the ground.

Cable drove slowly along the street in the residential neighborhood, nodding at people who gave him a friendly wave and a smile. He was patrolling the town, looking for any potential problems that might require the services of the sheriff.

That he was now turning onto his own street for

the third time was a fact that only he was aware of and was none too pleased about. But it seemed as though the Land Rover had a mind of its own, kept bringing him back here to see if Lindsey's vehicle was parked in his driveway.

Cable's hold on the steering wheel tightened and his muscles tensed as he saw a pickup truck at his house with a magnetic sign on the door advertising The Green Thumb nursery.

He pulled into the driveway behind the truck, turned off the ignition, then folded his arms on the top of the steering wheel and frowned.

Why was he here? he asked himself. Well, it didn't take a genius to figure out that he'd been cruising by his house with the hope of finding Lindsey there with lilac bush in tow.

But why? Surely he wasn't still reeling from a bruised ego because the rather mysterious Ms. Patterson had given him the cold shoulder. He wasn't still on that immature trip. Was he?

Hell, he didn't know, Cable thought, scooping up Buddy from the passenger seat and getting out of the vehicle. Maybe he *was* that much of a jerk, which would be rather unsettling to discover.

What he needed and was about to do, Cable thought, striding toward the gate to the backyard with Buddy tucked under one arm, was to see Lindsey Patterson again. He would realize that while, yes, she was an attractive woman, she was simply that—an attractive woman. One more among the multitudes.

With that information firmly in place in his beleaguered brain he would be able to dismiss Lindsey from his mind, would no longer be subjected to the heated desire that rocketed through his body when he dwelled on the image of her. He would get her into proper perspective and that would be that. Fine.

Cable entered the yard, then stopped dead in his tracks as his heart thundered.

Lindsey was facing away from him and was bent over at the waist as she placed a metal measuring tape along the ground. Her femininely rounded bottom was his for the viewing, as were her long, shapely legs, which were encased in formfitting jeans.

The dreaded heat slammed into him, then coiled low in his body. Cable swore under his breath, then set Buddy down on the grass. The puppy bolted toward Lindsey, yapping at high volume.

"Oh," Lindsey gasped.

She spun around, lost her balance and landed on her bottom on the grass with a thump. Cable hurried forward and extended one hand toward her.

"I'm sorry," he said. "I didn't mean to startle you, Lindsey. Are you hurt?"

"No, I'm...oh, gracious," Lindsey said, then laughed as Buddy jumped onto her lap and wiggled in obvious delight that she was down on his level and must be ready to play.

"Buddy, cut it out," Cable said.

Lindsey placed the dog on the grass, got to her feet and brushed her hands across her bottom.

"No, I'm not hurt," she said, smiling, "to answer your question."

Cable Montana was still drop-dead gorgeous. Her imagination hadn't played any tricks on her since she'd first seen him, that was for sure. But she told herself that her heart was racing from the unexpected intrusion while she was working, *not* as a result of seeing the sheriff again. "What are you doing here?"

Cable shoved his Stetson up with one thumb, a gesture so blatantly *male* that Lindsey felt a strange flutter in the pit of her stomach which changed rapidly into a thrumming heat that traveled throughout her.

"I live here," Cable said.

"I realize that, Sheriff Montana," Lindsey said, averting her eyes from his green...so incredibly green...ones. "But we agreed that you'd keep Buddy away from here while I was figuring out a plan of action to keep him from destroying your landscaping."

"I know, but I thought you might need some help, or…" Cable cleared his throat. "It's awfully warm out here and your cheeks are really pink. Would you like some iced tea?"

"Thank you for the offer, but I'm finished," Lindsey said, looking at Cable again. "I've planted the new bush and measured the area that needs protecting. I'll order the barrier when I get back to the nursery. It should be here in a few days. In the meantime, I suggest you keep an eye on the felon when he's in the yard."

"Yes, I'll certainly do that." Cable paused. "Can't you spare a few minutes for a cold drink? I'd hate to think that you got overheated from tackling my disaster here."

"Well, yes, okay," Lindsey said, nodding. She was overheated, but it wasn't from the sun. This man, this hunk-of-stuff man, was a menace. But she could handle this. No problem. She was once again in control. "A glass of iced tea sounds perfect, Sheriff Montana."

"Good," Cable said. "Let's go into the house. I need to stop at my vehicle and radio the office to let them know where I am. We might as well use the front door and get Buddy out of temptation's way."

"I'll collect my tools," Lindsey said.

"Let me carry them for you, Lindsey," Cable

said. "I'll put them in the back of your truck. Why don't you grab the furry beast? And, Lindsey? My name is Cable."

Lindsey nodded. "All right…Cable."

The tools were placed in the back of Lindsey's truck and Buddy was held securely in Lindsey's arms as the trio started across the front yard toward the small porch.

"Yoo-hoo, Sheriff Montana," a voice called.

Lindsey and Cable stopped and turned to see a woman in her late sixties hurrying toward them, carrying a wicker basket.

"Hello, Sheriff," the woman said. "Oh, hello to you, too, Lindsey. My goodness, what a sweet doggie. I heard you had a new member of the family, Sheriff."

"Yes, ma'am," Cable said.

"I won't keep you a second," the woman said. "I've brought your dinner, Sheriff. Actually, my daughter made it. She works at the library. Alida Ann Macintosh? Have you met my daughter yet, Sheriff?"

"I don't believe I've had the pleasure, ma'am," Cable said, mentally rolling his eyes heavenward.

"Oh, I know Alida Ann," Lindsey said, smiling brightly. "She has those twin boys, doesn't she? What are they now? Ten? Eleven years old?"

"They just turned thirteen," the woman said,

frowning. "Teenagers are such a handful, aren't they? Especially boys without a father. Alida Ann is beside herself about the behavior of the twins and…but enough of that. Alida Ann's specialty is her eggplant casserole, Sheriff, and she wanted you to sample it. So, I volunteered to bring it by for you and here I am."

"Eggplant?" Cable said, nearly choking on the word. "An eggplant casserole?"

"I've heard things about that eggplant casserole of Alida Ann's," Lindsey said pleasantly. "I'm sure it's delicious and that the sheriff will savor every bite of it for his evening meal. Wasn't that thoughtful of Alida Ann, Cable? To send you over an eggplant casserole?"

Cable narrowed his eyes and in the next instant whipped one arm around Lindsey's shoulders and pulled her close to his side. Lindsey gasped in surprise and nearly dropped Buddy.

"Very thoughtful," Cable said, no hint of a smile on his face. "We'll enjoy it together, won't we…sweetheart? Oh, yes, we'll eat it by candlelight tonight. It will be very romantic."

"Oh, my stars," Alida Ann's mother said, her eyes widening.

Lindsey attempted to wiggle out of Cable's grasp, but he tightened his hold on her shoulders.

"Well, what can I say?" Cable said with an exaggerated sigh. "I guess our little secret is a secret no longer, my dearest Lindsey. The whole town will soon know that you and I are…are an item."

"I…" Lindsey started.

"I must dash," the woman said, shoving the basket at Cable and forcing him to grab the handle. "Wait until I tell…oh. Goodbye. Have a nice day and…and romantic night and…goodbye."

"Goodbye," Cable said breezily.

The woman scurried away and Cable chuckled as he dropped his arm from Lindsey's shoulders. She stepped backward and planted her hands on her hips.

"Cable Montana," she said, her dark eyes flashing with anger, "say your final farewell to Buddy because, mister, you are a dead man."

## Chapter Three

Cable opened his mouth to reply to Lindsey's threat. In the next instant he snapped his jaws closed again as he realized that the only thing available in his mind for him to say was that when Lindsey Patterson was angry, she was absolutely, sensationally gorgeous.

"I...am...leaving," Lindsey said, her words slow and measured and laced with fury. She shoved Buddy at Cable, forcing him to wrap his free arm around the wiggling puppy while holding the handle of the wicker basket in his other hand. "Goodbye."

Lindsey started toward her truck and Cable shook his head slightly to bring himself back to the disastrous moment and out of his very close to passion laden haze.

"Lindsey, wait," he said, spinning around. "Let me explain what I said, what I did."

"No," she said, not slowing her steps.

"Please? Five minutes? One cool glass of iced tea and five more minutes of your time? Please?"

Lindsey hesitated, then stopped, her back to Cable. She turned and looked at him, curbing a smile as she saw him struggling with Buddy, who was determined to discover what was in the fascinating basket.

"Five minutes and not one minute more," she said, lifting her chin. "Oh, good heavens, do you realize what you've done? I could just scream." She paused. "Aaak," she yelled, causing Cable to cringe. "There. I *did* scream and feel better for it, thank you very much."

"Whatever works," Cable said, smiling weakly. "Let's go into the house. All right?"

"Five minutes," Lindsey repeated. She closed the distance between them and took Buddy from Cable. "Give me that dog before he takes a nose-dive into the eggplant casserole." She shuddered. "Yuck. Eggplant."

As Lindsey headed for the front porch of Cable's house he was right behind her.

"That's it, don't you see?" he said. "It was the eggplant that pushed me over the edge. I was already teetering because of the tuna fish, you know what I mean? Then, cripes, an eggplant casserole and…and I just lost it, Lindsey."

"Mmm," she said, glaring at him as he moved past her to unlock the front door.

Inside the house, Lindsey swept her gaze over the living room and mentally nodded in approval.

Nice, she thought, very nice. The furniture was sturdy and masculine, done in a brown-and-tan tweed, and the tables were oak. There was a small flagstone fireplace banked by bookcases that were filled to overflowing.

No dirty dishes cluttering up the place, she noted, but there was a plaid flannel shirt tossed over the back of the sofa, giving the room a tidy but lived-in look. She liked Cable's cozy little house.

She was not, however, going to stand there and chitchat about Sheriff Montana's home. It was going to take her total concentration to keep from strangling the man with her bare hands.

"Have a seat," Cable said. "Oh, you can put Buddy down, too. I'll get rid of this…this thing in the basket and get us a cool drink."

Lindsey set Buddy on the floor, then sank onto the sofa that was facing the fireplace and folded her arms beneath her breasts as Cable disappeared in the direction, she assumed, of the kitchen. Buddy curled up in a puddle of sunlight by the front window and went to sleep.

A fireplace, she mused, staring at it. That was one thing she was lacking in the house she was renting. Her place was on the other side of town. It was only a few years old, and didn't have the charm of Cable's older home.

A fireplace. On a cold winter night with big, lazy flakes of snow falling outside, the warming flames in the hearth would beckon, inviting Cable and…and someone to settle by the fire with…brandy? No, that was too big-city yuppie.

Steaming mugs of hot chocolate with melting marshmallows. Yes, that's what they'd have—hot chocolate with marshmallows.

They wouldn't turn on the lamps on the end tables, just sit within the magical circle of light created by the leaping flames.

The hot chocolate would warm them down to their toes. Toes that had been freezing cold because they'd been outside in the snow, building a funny snowman together, laughing like carefree children.

The drinks would be consumed and marshmallow mustaches…licked away by the other's tongue before their lips met in a searing kiss and then...then Cable would slide his strong but gentle hands beneath her sweater and murmur in her ear that he wanted her, desired her, wished to make love to her and she would whisper—

"Iced tea," Cable said, coming back into the room carrying two glasses.

Lindsey jerked as Cable's deep, rumbling voice shattered the sensuous images.

She felt a flush of embarrassment creep onto her cheeks. What on earth was the matter with her? She sat in front of an empty fireplace on a warm summer day and fantasized about a cold winter night and hot chocolate and Cable Montana, and kisses shared and—

She didn't engage in nonsense like this. She was a twenty-eight-year-old mature woman, not a dewy-eyed adolescent. She didn't remember ever having sexual daydreams like that one when she *was* a dewy-eyed adolescent, for Pete's sake.

Lindsey Patterson, she ordered herself, get a grip...on that glass of iced tea that Cable Montana had been standing there offering her for the past three years.

"Thank you," she mumbled, taking the glass.

"You're welcome," Cable said, then sank onto the other end of the sofa. He shifted slightly so he could look directly at Lindsey. "I'm very sorry about what I said and did outside in front of Mrs…whatever her name is…Alida Ann's mother.''

''The eggplant made you do it,'' Lindsey said, smiling in spite of herself.

''That's exactly right,'' Cable said with a burst of laughter. ''Man, can you imagine buying one of those ugly, lumpy purple things in the produce department of the grocery store, taking it home, then—no, I can't think about it or I'll give myself nightmares. Eggplant casserole. It was the last straw, Lindsey. I just…''

''Lost it,'' Lindsey said, frowning. ''So you said. But that doesn't erase the damage you've done. I hate to think how many people already have the news bulletin that you and I are a couple, are…together.''

''Yeah, I know.''

Cable drained his drink in four swallows, then plunked the empty glass onto the end table next to the sofa. He got to his feet and began to pace back and forth in front of the fireplace.

Lindsey took a sip of the delicious iced tea, then watched Cable as he continued his trek. He ran one hand over his chin, then shoved his fingers through his thick, dark hair.

Such masculine mannerisms, Lindsey thought, her gaze riveted on Cable. The man just didn't quit.

And to top it off, he looked like a million dollars in his sheriff's uniform. The crisp tan material was stretched tightly over his wide shoulders and broad chest, and the matching trousers hugged long, muscled legs and, shame on her, a very nice tush.

A gold star-shaped badge was pinned to the pocket of Cable's shirt, and a holstered gun was strapped around his narrow hips.

Cable Montana was the quintessential western sheriff, and her heart was beating like a bongo drum because of the picture he presented as he walked back and forth in front of her.

Lindsey took a deep swallow of her drink and told herself that the liquid was cooling her off from the sun...nothing else.

Cable stopped abruptly and looked directly at Lindsey. One second went by, then two, then three...

"What!" Lindsey said finally.

"I have a plan," Cable said. "It's a tad off-the-wall, but it just might work. Will you listen to me with an open mind? Hear me out?"

Lindsey set her glass on the end table, folded her arms beneath her breasts, hesitated, then nodded.

"Thank you," Cable said. "Lindsey, you said that the matchmakers did their number on you and finally gave up, decided you were a hopeless case. Right?''

''Right,'' she said, nodding.

''Which means, I assume, that you have no desire to get married, or even become seriously involved with a man. You apparently like your life just as it is, value your independence. Right?''

It was much more complex than that, Lindsey thought, but she wasn't about to bare her soul, share her innermost secrets with Cable, or anyone else. Not now, not ever.

''Close enough,'' she said. ''What's your point?''

Cable sat down sideways next to Lindsey and perched one arm on the top of the sofa behind her.

Those really were the greenest eyes she'd ever seen, Lindsey thought. And the darkest, longest lashes. And the—

''Okay, look,'' Cable said.

Oh, I am, Lindsey thought dreamily. She could spend all week *looking* at Cable Montana's incredible eyes.

''Lindsey?''

''What? Oh! Yes! I'm listening, Cable.''

''Good,'' he said, nodding. ''I don't want to get married, either. Not again. I did that bit and it was a disaster I don't care to repeat. I'm single and intend to stay that way. We're on the same wave-length on the subject.''

''So?''

''So, the matchmakers are driving me out of my ever-lovin' mind,'' Cable said. ''I can't take any more of this nonsense they're dishing out.''

''They're dishing out tuna-fish and eggplant cas-seroles,'' Lindsey said, laughing. She sobered in the next instant when Cable glared at her. ''Sorry. Couldn't resist. Carry on. However, I have to admit I have no idea what you're leading up to here.''

''It's really quite simple,'' he said. ''Simple, but close to genius-level thinking.''

''Don't break your arm patting yourself on the back, Cable,'' Lindsey said, rolling her eyes heav-enward.

Cable chuckled and Lindsey felt a shiver slither down her spine as she heard the oh-so-sexy sound.

''How can someone who has just dug a hole and planted a bush and crawled around on the ground in the hot summer sun smell so good?'' Cable said suddenly. ''Like…like wildflowers.''

''I beg your pardon?'' Lindsey said, her eyes widening as she ignored the funny little two-step her heart was in the process of doing.

''Oh. I got off track for a second.'' Cable paused. ''But you really do smell like wildflowers, Lindsey. It's nice. Very nice.''

"Thank you," she said, deciding she'd had quite enough of gazing into the fathomless depths of Cable's sea-green eyes. She stared at the badge on his shirt pocket. "Your genius-level plan?"

"Oh, yeah." Cable cleared his throat and mentally ordered the heat that was rocketing through his body to take a hike. But, damn it, Lindsey really did smell good. "You and I know that we're not interested in, nor intend to become involved in, a serious relationship.

"However, due to my outburst in front of Alida Ann's mother, which was caused by my weakened mental faculties, which are the result of the attack on my person by the matchmakers and—"

"Cable, you're not testifying in a court of law, for heaven's sake," Lindsey said, looking into his eyes again. "Just spit it out."

"Right. By tonight, at the latest, the town will be buzzing," Cable said. "The word will be out that you and I are…are…"

"I get the picture. So?"

"So, my lovely Lindsey," Cable said, smiling, "my plan is that we go with the flow, pretend to be a couple who are, yes, indeed, very seriously involved with each other."

Lindsey jumped to her feet, then spun around and stared at Cable.

"Are you crazy?" she said none too quietly. "That's it, isn't it? You're certifiably insane."

Cable got to his feet and gripped Lindsey's shoulders. "No, I'm not nuts," he said, a frantic edge to his voice. "I will be if one more casserole is plunked on my front porch, but I'm still hanging on by a thread here. Lindsey, please, just think about it, would you? If the matchmakers think we're together, having a really hot and heavy—"

"Hot and heavy?" Lindsey shrieked.

"Erase that. It was a figure of speech. They'll believe that we're involved with each other. We'll be seen around town in each other's company, have dinner out, go to a movie, attend this and that...whatever. We'll know it's all a charade, but the matchmakers will probably have a bash to celebrate their victory and that will be the end of the tuna-fish and eggplant. Get it? Great, huh?"

"Oh, yes, it's just a ducky plan, Cable," Lindsey said, her voice ringing with sarcasm. "But aren't you leaving out a tiny little detail?"

"Like what?" he said, dropping his hands from her shoulders.

"How long do you think we would have to keep up this charade?" Lindsey said. "And when we end the phony performance, what's to keep them from starting the casserole and cookies bit again?"

"I've already thought of that," Cable said, appearing extremely pleased with himself. "Our romance is over. It's kaput. Finished. Didn't work out. We're really bummed, so very sad and heartbroken, and any further matchmaking would be more than we could emotionally bear.

"The matchmakers leave us in peace to lick our wounds and relive our memories of the happy times we spent together. They continue with the attack on whoever they'd zeroed in on when it became known we were an item. There. That covers it."

"Oh," Lindsey said, nodding slowly. "That's not bad, not bad at all." She paused. "Darn it, Cable, this isn't fair. I suffered through the matchmaker's nonsense and earned my title of being a hopeless case. Now you've thrown me right back into the thick of things because of what you did and said in front of Alida Ann's mother."

"I know that and this will make up for what I did to you," Cable said. "You'll help me and I'll be able to rectify the misery-waiting-to-happen that I brought down on you. Ah, please, Lindsey? I'm a desperate man. I'm not above begging. Want me to beg? Just say the word and I'll beg."

"Oh, for heaven's sake," Lindsey said, laughing.

"Will you do it? Pretend to be my significant

other? Go along with the charade? It'll get us both off the hook, don't you see?''

"How long do you think we'd have to keep up this sham?'' Lindsey said, frowning.

Cable lifted one shoulder in a shrug. "I don't have a clue. A couple of weeks? Three, four, at the most? I don't know. But then? Ah, the sweet bliss of peacefulness, of being left alone to go about our lives as we so choose. No more tuna fish. No more eggplant. No more coconut fig cookies.''

"Give me a minute to think this over,'' Lindsey said.

"Take all the time you need,'' Cable said, sitting down on the sofa.

Lindsey took up the same pacing path that Cable had used and he watched her trek back and forth in front of the fireplace, his head swiveling as though he was observing a tennis match.

Well, Lindsey? she asked herself. What's it going to be? Yes? No?

Heaven knows she didn't want to endure another onslaught by the matchmakers. Oh, perish the thought.

Cable's wacky plan had merit, it really did. It was so nuts that it just might work.

And, it would be rather nice to have a few dates, to get all dressed up and go out to dinner, to see a movie, whatever. There would be none of the usual singles-scene malarkey, either. The uncomfortable moment at her front door when her escort brought her home just wouldn't come into play because the whole thing would be a charade.

She would invite Cable in for a nightcap to keep up appearances, but she wouldn't have to worry that he would attempt to hustle her into bed with him. She'd bid him adieu a short time later and that would be that until they went somewhere together again.

Mmm, Lindsey mused, as she continued to pace. The only negative thing she could find in this crazy scenario was her own silly, sensual reaction to Cable's masculine magnetism.

Masculine magnetism? That was a tad much, but she knew what she meant. She had overreacted to him on a man and woman plane almost from the moment she'd met him, had even indulged in a nonsensical fantasy about licking marshmallow mustaches off each other and—

He was just a man, and she could handle this just fine. Granted, he was much *more* of a man than she was accustomed to but, hey, she was a mature woman, not a naive child.

Lindsey stopped, turned to face Cable, then drew a steadying breath.

"Yes, okay," she said, nodding. "I'll go along with this charade of yours, Cable."

Cable punched one fist in the air, then got to his feet. "That's great, Lindsey. I really appreciate it and it's going to work, no doubt about it."

"I hope so," Lindsey said. "I certainly don't want to be the target of the matchmakers again."

"I know what you mean. We'll start tonight if that's satisfactory with you. I'll pick you up at eight o'clock and we'll go to dinner at Hamilton House. The restaurant in the hotel is a very popular spot and we'll be on display for a great many people."

"Tonight?" she said. "Well, I suppose there's no sense in delaying getting this show on the road. I insist on paying for my own meal, though."

"No way," Cable said, frowning. "In the first place, I'm an old-fashioned guy when it comes to picking up the tab when I'm out with a woman.

"And second, if it wasn't for me, you wouldn't be in this mess. Buying you dinner is the least I can do. You're going to be giving up your quiet leisure hours at home after work for a while."

"Oh, well, I..."

"Hopefully this charade won't last too long," Cable went on. "Down the road we'll be able to tell if the dear ladies are no longer paying any attention to us and have moved on to fresher prey."

"Right," Lindsey said, frowning slightly. "Just a few weeks or so should do the trick."

"Yep, then you can pick up your life where you left off and things will be back to normal for you." Cable glanced at his watch. "I have to get back on patrol. I'll see you tonight."

"Eight o'clock," Lindsey said, starting toward the door.

"Oh, cripes," Cable said, scooping up Buddy from where he was still snoozing in the circle of sunlight. "What am I going to do with this boy tonight?"

"Don't leave him in the backyard alone," Lindsey said, laughing as she opened the front door. "You'll end up buying another lilac bush if you do. Maybe you should hire a baby-sitter."

"There's a thought," Cable said, following Lindsey to the porch.

"I was kidding," she said.

"Oh. Well, I'll think of something," Cable said as he locked the door.

The sound of a car horn reached them and they turned to look at the street. A woman was driving by slowly, waving and smiling.

"Wave," Cable said, lifting one hand in a greeting to the woman. "The curtain, Ms. Patterson, just went up."

## Chapter Four

Just before eight o'clock that night, Cable drove slowly in the direction of Lindsey's house, attempting to gather his scattered thoughts and make some sense of the muddled mess that had once been his fairly proficient mind.

He was, he admitted to himself, confused as hell over the sense of anticipation that had steadily built within him during the afternoon and early evening at the prospect of seeing Lindsey Patterson that night and taking her to dinner at Hamilton House.

He'd even spent a ridiculous amount of time choosing what he would wear and had changed his mind three times regarding the selection of a tie. He'd finally gotten himself decked out in a dark brown suit, tan shirt and brown paisley-print tie.

He ran one hand down the tie in question and wondered if his attire was basically boring.

In the next instant he smacked the steering wheel with the heel of one hand in self-disgust. This was not, he told himself for the umpteenth time, a date, in the normal sense of the word. But even if it was, he hadn't behaved like a nervous, inexperienced teenager when he'd been an inexperienced teenager. Why was he such a wreck at his worldly old age of thirty-seven, for crying out loud?

He took a deep, steadying breath and let it out with a puff of his cheeks.

It wasn't the dinner date with Lindsey, that was throwing him off-kilter, he suddenly realized, it was the *circumstances* under which he and Lindsey were operating. *The charade.*

He had going-onstage-in-front-of-an-audience nerves regarding the evening ahead, that was all.

"That's it," Cable said with a rush of relief as he pulled into Lindsey's driveway and turned off the ignition to the Land Rover.

After he'd gotten out of the vehicle, he stopped for a moment to sweep his gaze over Lindsey's small, fairly new house. He couldn't see all the details of Lindsey's home in the glow of the street-light at the curb, but he got the impression that it was well cared for and…cute, for lack of a better adjective. Lindsey had chosen to live in a growing part of Prescott that boasted newer homes, while he'd zeroed in on the older section of town.

Frowning and running one hand over his chin, he cut across the colored gravel that made up the front yard of the house. He and Lindsey had certainly chosen opposite types of places to call home, that was for sure. What other differences did they have? Were they totally incompatible?

Oh, for cripes sake, he thought, as he knocked on the front door of Lindsey's house, it didn't matter if he and Lindsey couldn't agree on something as simple as the weather.

They would be *pretending* to be a match made in heaven, would simply bluff if it came to light that they were poles apart in attitudes and opinions. The trick was to convince those who were observing them that they were soul mates, having discovered each other at long last.

The matchmaking multitudes just had to buy into this charade, then leave the brokenhearted couple alone as they nursed their wounds when the whole affair blew up and was history.

Affair? Cable's mind echoed. He'd do well to remove that word from his vocabulary for the duration of this endeavor. An affair hinted at sex, long nights of torrid lovemaking and—

Heat rocketed through Cable and he clenched his jaw as he knocked on the door with more force than was necessary.

"Coming, coming," Lindsey said, hurrying down the hallway from her bedroom. She stopped in the middle of the living room and drew a steadying breath.

Calm down, she told herself. She'd been all ready to go half an hour ago, then had suddenly decided she didn't like the dress she'd chosen to wear and had returned to her closet to start over.

Dumb, really dumb. It wouldn't matter if she wore a gunnysack for this outing, because it wasn't a date, it was a performance. And now Sheriff Cable Montana was pounding on her front door, but it wasn't really Cable, the man, who was there to pick her up, it was Cable, the actor, who would escort her to dinner.

"I can handle this," Lindsey said, splaying one hand on her fluttering stomach. "I'm fine. And this nutty charade will work. It has to, for the sake of my sanity and Cable's. We will have victory over the matchmakers."

Lindsey nodded decisively, marched to the door and flung it open.

Then she just stood there, drinking in the sight of gorgeous Cable in his suit and tie, having no idea if she'd remembered to say "Hello."

Oh, hell, Cable thought, as his mind catalogued every detail of the vision of loveliness before him. He'd enjoyed looking at Lindsey when she'd been wearing jeans and a T-shirt. But Lindsey in a silky looking ice-blue dress that fell in soft folds to just below her knees, floated across her breasts, nipped in at her tiny waist, was almost too much to take. Man, oh, man, she was beautiful. Had he said "Hello," or hadn't he managed to get past gawking at her?

"Hello," they said in unison.

Lindsey sighed. "Please come in, Cable."

"Thank you," he said.

Lindsey closed the door behind him and he scrutinized the small living room. Lindsey had decorated in white wicker furniture with puffy cushions splashed with big, bright flowers on a white background. The carpet was pale mint-green, and plantation shutters covered the front window.

"This is nice," Cable said, nodding. "It's like a stroll in a garden."

Lindsey laughed. "Befitting a woman who owns a plant nursery. I hardly have time to tend to plants here, so I fake it." She paused and frowned. "Which I seem to be doing a lot of lately. Cable,

I'm a wreck. I've never in my entire life pretended to be...be...whatever it is we're supposed to be.''

"Hey, don't feel alone," Cable said. "This is a first for me, too. We just have to remember what's at stake here, Lindsey. If we can pull this off, we'll be free to get on with our lives as we choose to live them." He paused. "You look fantastic, by the way."

"Oh, well, thank you," she said. "You're rather dashing yourself. I'll get my purse and then we can go. Oh, what did you end up doing with Buddy?"

"He's set up in the laundry room at my house. Food, water, toys, newspapers, the whole nine yards. He should be fine. At least there are no lilac bushes in that room to dig up. I doubt if he'll attack the washing machine."

"There's a thought," Lindsey said, laughing. "But I wouldn't want to put any money on it."

As Lindsey crossed in front of Cable to retrieve her purse from a small table, he nearly groaned when he caught the aroma of her perfume, a lovely, light fragrance he couldn't identify but caused a hot fist to tighten in his gut.

If he didn't get his testosterone under control right now, he thought, this was going to be a very long evening.

It was a picture-perfect summer night in the mile-high little town, with millions of sparkling stars in the black-velvet sky and the aroma of flowers and pine trees wafting through the cool air.

As Cable drove away from Lindsey's house, she noticed the two-way radio under the dashboard of the Land Rover and the rifle in brackets behind the seat.

"Are you on duty tonight?" she said to Cable. "I mean, this is the sheriff's official vehicle, isn't it?"

"Yes, it is," Cable said, nodding. "It's part of the deal of being the sheriff here. They provide my transportation, but it sort of puts me in a position of being available twenty-four seven. I'm not on the duty roster tonight, though."

"So you never really have a day off?"

"Sure I do," he said, smiling over at her quickly. "Prescott isn't exactly a high-crime city, you know. Plus, I have a very well-trained team of deputies backing me up. It sure beats working for the department I was with in Nevada." He nodded. "I like living in Prescott very much. If the good citizens cast their votes as I hope they will down the road, I intend to stay here."

"I'm certain they'll reelect you until you're old and feeble," Lindsey said, smiling.

"We'll see. What brought you to Prescott, Lindsey?"

"I was working at a nursery in Los Angeles and

was ready to branch out on my own, take the big plunge,'' she said. She'd needed to escape from the painful memories of... No. ''I decided to look at small towns in California, Arizona, New Mexico, as I'd had enough of big-city living. I drove into Prescott and knew I was home. That was three years ago and I can't imagine ever leaving.''

''Do you have family somewhere?'' Cable said.

''No,'' she said quietly. ''I was a late-in-life surprise for my parents. They've passed away. There aren't any other relatives, either. It's just little ol' me and The Green Thumb.'' She paused. ''What about you, Cable? Is there a bunch of Montanas somewhere?''

''Besides my ex-wife?'' he said. ''She doesn't count. She took back her maiden name after the divorce. She said she didn't want to go through life sounding like a godforsaken state, or a retired football player.'' He shrugged. ''Whatever.

''But there are Montanas. My parents are retired and live in Florida. My dad fishes and my mother plays bridge. They're lovin' it.

''I have a brother in Florida, too, who is two years younger than I am. He teaches third grade, is married and has three boys, who my folks spoil rotten. They all have a good time together down there. I visit them when I get the chance.''

"Your family sounds lovely," Lindsey said, a rather wistful tone to her voice. "I wish I hadn't been an only child, but..." She shrugged. "Well, we're all caught up on each other's backgrounds. I'm sorry you had a disastrous marriage."

"It was a mistake from day one," he said. "She liked the flash and dash of my uniform, the authority I had, but the hours I put in got old very fast. She wanted me to quit. I refused, because giving up my career would be like losing a huge part of who I am. It got nasty and...end of story.

"I came away from that nightmare knowing that I would never marry again. When you put your heart and soul into a relationship, try to make it work, give it all you have and it falls apart, it just rips you up. I'm not going through that again. Nope. No way."

"You sound a tad bitter, Cable," Lindsey said.

"I don't mean to. I like to think I'm wiser, that's all." Cable paused and frowned as he realized he'd just revealed his innermost secrets to a woman he hardly knew. "That's my tale of woe and the reason I'm running from the matchmakers of Prescott. Why are you so determined to stay single?"

Oh, wouldn't it be nice, so freeing, to just pour out her heart to Cable, Lindsey thought, tell him the truth of why she would not, could not, ever marry? How strange it was to suddenly have the desire to share her secret with this man. It didn't make sense really. She barely knew Cable Montana, but yet...

"Lindsey?"

"What? Oh, I'm just set in my ways, and terribly independent. Plus I put in long hours at The Green Thumb and there's very little time left to devote to any type of relationship. It wouldn't be fair to someone I might become involved with." Lindsey shook her head. "No, I'm single and intend to stay that way."

"There is such a thing as compromise, you know." Cable laughed and shook his head. "Listen to me, the great wizard of how to make marriage work. That's a joke. I *couldn't* compromise, give up my chosen profession to *maybe* save my marriage. You obviously know what's best for you, just as I do. Now if we can convince the matchmakers that we're doing fine being footloose and fancy-free after our broken hearts mend when our relationship dissolves into dust, we'll have it made. There's Hamilton House up ahead. I hope you're hungry."

"I'm starving and I know how delicious the food is at the hotel," Lindsey said. "When they appear with that dessert cart, I go nuts."

"Temptation thy name is chocolate?" Cable said.

"Bingo."

Cable parked and came around to assist Lindsey from the vehicle. As they walked along the sidewalk toward the front doors of Hamilton House, Cable's words echoed in Lindsey's mind.

*You obviously know what's best for you.*

No, Cable, Lindsey thought. The truth of the matter was that she knew what she had to settle for. A life alone. She continually strived to maintain a sense of inner peace and contentment, an acceptance of how things were. But sometimes, despite her very best efforts, she was just so very lonely.

A genuine smile formed on Lindsey's lips as they entered the lobby of the hotel.

"I love to come in here," she said. "It's like stepping back in time to the turn of the century. Brandon did such a fantastic job restoring this old place."

"You know Brandon and Andrea?" Cable said.

"Oh, yes. They've been regular customers of mine ever since their house was built. They're putting together a lovely landscaping plan, including a grassy area in the backyard where Ashley can play. It's hard to believe that their daughter is fifteen months old already. She is a cutie-pie."

"That she is," Cable said, nodding. "She's got me wrapped around her little finger. She is—hey, speaking of Brandon, there he is, just getting out of the elevator.'' He frowned. ''Ben's with him and the good doctor is carrying his medical bag. Something must be going on here.''

''Oh, dear.''

Cable and Lindsey walked past the corridor leading to the dining room to meet Brandon and Ben in the middle of the lobby. Greetings were exchanged and Cable realized from what was said that Lindsey also knew Ben Rizzoli and his wife, Megan.

It would seem, Cable thought, that just about everyone he knew had already met Lindsey Patterson except him. Well, thanks to Buddy and the poor lilac bush, the sheriff of Prescott knew Lindsey Patterson now, too. He just might give the puppy an extra chewy treat to thank him for that fact.

''Seeing you here with your medical bag looks rather ominous, Ben,'' Cable said. ''Is something wrong?''

''Aunt Charity has a stubborn cold,'' Ben said. ''She actually admitted that she felt rotten enough to go to bed, which brought me running. I'm going to be keeping a close eye on her.''

''Oh, goodness,'' Lindsey said, ''I'm so sorry to hear that Aunt Charity isn't well. Aunt Prudence must be so worried. They're such wonderful ladies. I adore them both.''

"Everyone does,'' Brandon said, chuckling. "They may be twin sisters, but they're so different it's a hoot. Aunt Prudence is so prim and proper, and Aunt Charity? Well, she's something else. She just told me to get my butt home where I belonged and leave her in peace.''

"That sounds like Aunt Charity,'' Cable said, smiling. "She does speak her mind.''

"In spades,'' Brandon said. "But Ben nailed it. For Aunt Charity to take to her bed means she's really under the weather. I forget at times that my great-aunts aren't spring chickens any longer. They're just such an important part of my life and...well, hell, enough gloomy talk. Aunt Charity will bounce back from this cold and be as good as new. Right, Ben?''

"You bet,'' Ben said. "So, Lindsey, Cable, are you two here for dinner?''

Lindsey and Cable nodded.

"One of my afternoon patients today mentioned that the sheriff had...how did that go—'' Ben squinted up at the ceiling ''—oh, yeah, the sheriff had 'taken up' with that pretty little gal that has the plant nursery.''

"Only *one* patient told you that?'' Cable said,

raising his eyebrows. "The grapevine must be slipping."

"I had a light afternoon scheduled," Ben said, chuckling. "I'm sure I'll hear plenty tomorrow about this dinner you two are about to share. You're really asking for it by coming to Hamilton House. You should have driven over to Flagstaff."

"No problem," Cable said. "Let the tongues wag. Well, gentlemen, Ms. Patterson and I have a table waiting. I'll be checking with you, Ben, to see how Aunt Charity is doing."

"So will I," Lindsey said. "Good night, Ben, Brandon. Say hello to Megan and Andrea for me, and give Ashley a tickle, too, Brandon."

"Enjoy your dinner," Brandon said.

"Yeah," Ben said, "enjoy."

"We will," Cable said, as they started toward the dining room. "We most definitely will."

The salads were crisp and crunchy, the steaks thick and succulent, the baked potatoes fluffy and swimming in butter and sour cream, the wine smooth and warming, and the conversation flowed easily from one topic to the next throughout the delicious meal.

She was, Lindsey thought, as the waiter placed wafer-thin snifters of brandy and fine-china cups of coffee on the table, having a marvelous time.

The butterflies in her stomach had zoomed off into oblivion and she'd totally relaxed. That was after she'd gotten used to the very interested glances being slid in her and Cable's direction and the whispered conversations she could see taking place when their presence in the dining room became known.

Yes, she was thoroughly enjoying herself in the company of the handsome and attentive sheriff. Goodness, it had been a long time since she'd felt so...so special, made to feel that everything she said was of extreme importance. Cable certainly was a master at making a woman feel...well, womanly. It was nice...very, very nice.

Cable lifted his snifter of brandy into the air. "To us and our goal."

"Amen," Lindsey said, smiling as she touched her snifter to his, then took a sip of the amber liquid. "Mmm. What a perfect finish to a marvelous dinner. I am so full, I don't think I'll need to eat anything for a week. It was the Black Forest cake that did me in. Did you see the size of that serving?"

"I did," Cable said, nodding. "I also saw you eat every bite of it."

Lindsey laughed. "I know. I'm such a piggy, but it was so-o-o sinfully rich and yummy."

"I like to hear you laugh," Cable said, looking

directly into Lindsey's eyes. "You laugh like you really mean it…nothing forced or phony…and it's a lovely sound, it really is."

"Well, thank you, Cable," Lindsey said. "No one has ever commented on my…well, my laugh before. That was a very nice thing to say." She paused. "I've enjoyed this evening so much." She raised her snifter in the air again. "To good food, good company."

Cable clinked his snifter against Lindsey's, then they took swallows of the rich brandy, their gazes meeting over the edges of the glasses.

Something shifted, changed. The muted conversations in the room disappeared, along with the noise of dishes being cleared and china cups being set onto saucers. A sensual mist seemed to materialize, weaving around them, creating a world that encompassed only the two of them.

Hearts began to beat with rapid tempos and the warmth from the brandy heightened the heat of desire that began to swirl within them, low and deep.

Oh, my, Lindsey thought dreamily, she was being consumed by the heat of…of passion, of desire in its purest and most honest form. She wanted this man, this incredible man, wanted to make love with him.

"Good evening, Sheriff," a voice said.

Lindsey jerked in her chair as the room came

back into focus. She looked up to see a man she didn't know standing by the table.

"What?" Cable said, then cleared his throat. "Oh, hello, Norm. Have you met Lindsey Patterson?"

"Haven't had the pleasure," Norm said.

Cable heard himself make the needed social introductions, while part of his mind was willing his body back under his command.

Whew, he thought. Something weird had happened all of a sudden there. He'd been going up in flames...big time, could still feel the hot coil low in his body.

His heart had been thudding like a bongo drum, and there had been only one thought hammering against his mind—he wanted Lindsey Patterson.

With an intensity beyond anything he could remember, he desired her, envisioned making sweet, slow love to her through the long hours of the night.

*This* was not part of the plan, not by a long shot. He had to get a grip right now.

"...make an official report, Cable," Norm was saying. "I'm not sitting still for this kind of vandalism. It's only a mailbox but, by damn, it's *my* mailbox, and I have to replace it. I'll come by your office tomorrow and fill out whatever paperwork is necessary. I want those yahoos caught and disciplined."

"You bet," Cable said, having no idea what had been done to Norm's mailbox.

"They did the same thing to Harvey Clink's mailbox, you know," Norm rattled on. "Smashed it to smithereens just like they did to mine. Probably used a baseball bat, or a piece of pipe. It's kids, bored teenagers, or whatever. You best catch those delinquents, Sheriff."

"I'll make it my top priority," Cable said, nodding. "Why don't you tell Harvey to come by the office and fill out a report, too?"

"I'll do that," Norm said. "Well, I'll leave you to finish your meal. The wife said I shouldn't be interrupting lovebirds like you two about my mailbox, but I said that you were the sheriff and I had the right to report the destruction of my property. Besides, it's early yet. You lovebirds have plenty of evening left to be alone. Good night. Pleasure meeting you, Ms. Patterson."

"Bye, Norm," Cable said.

"Goodbye," Lindsey said.

As Norm returned to his table, Lindsey leaned slightly forward.

"Lovebirds?" she whispered. "This is the first time we've been seen together in public, Cable, and we're already lovebirds?"

Cable chuckled. "Our plan is working even better than I hoped. At this rate we won't have to keep up this charade very long at all.''

''Oh.'' Lindsey nodded. ''Yes, you're probably right.'' That was *not* disappointment that was causing a cold knot to tighten in her tummy. No, it certainly wasn't. ''Well, that's good, isn't it?''

No, damn it, it wasn't good, Cable thought. The thought of ending the time spent with Lindsey before it had hardly begun was *not* setting well.

''Then again,'' he said, ''we don't want to take any chances. Norm's wife is just one woman referring to us as lovebirds. Just one. Our work is far from being completed, Lindsey.''

The cold twist in Lindsey's stomach was replaced by a warmth that spread throughout her.

''That's true,'' she said, smiling. ''The battle has just begun, Sheriff Montana. The war has not been won. Why don't I cook dinner for you tomorrow night? Your vehicle will be seen in my driveway.''

''That's an excellent idea,'' Cable said, matching her smile. ''Hey, look on the bright side. I'll be right there ready to leap into sheriffdom action in case someone attacks your mailbox.''

Their mingled laughter danced through the air, causing smiles to form on the faces of the diners observing Lindsey and Cable...the lovebirds.

## Chapter Five

The next afternoon Cable glanced up from the report he was reading at his desk as he heard the rap of knuckles on the open door to his office. A deputy was standing in the doorway with several sheets of paper in one hand.

"Hey, Mick," Cable said. "Come on in. What have you got?"

The young officer settled onto one of the chairs opposite the desk. Cable leaned back in the creaking leather chair and laced his fingers behind his head.

"Four reports so far," Mick said, "on smashed-up mailboxes. In my day we soaped windows, for cripes sake, and that was usually only on Halloween.''

"Yeah, well, times have changed," Cable said. "Is there any pattern to the locations of the damage?"

"Not really," Mick said, glancing at the reports. "These are pretty well scattered around town. The only thing consistent is that they're picking areas that don't have streetlights, the rotten little devils."

Cable frowned. "It's bored kids with not enough to do with school being out for the summer. We've got to nab them, though, before they hit any more, or get cockier and go for bigger price tag items. Let's do heavier patrol after dark in areas with no streetlights and hope we get lucky. I'll do an extra shift tonight and cruise through some neighborhoods."

"Oh, well, I'm sure the rest of the guys will do double time with me and cover this, Cable," Mick said. "There's no need for you to gum up your evening."

Cable shifted forward, picked up a pencil and tapped the eraser absently on the file on his desk.

"I don't ask more of you deputies than I'm willing to do myself, Mick," he said. "You know that."

"Well, yeah, sure, but that was before you were

involved with...what I mean is, I imagine you would rather be with...all I'm trying to say is..."

"Hold it," Cable said, raising one hand. "You're about as subtle as a rock. What you're fumble-mouthing about is that you figure I'd prefer to be with Lindsey Patterson tonight than out driving around trying to snag some kids who are getting their kicks by clobbering mailboxes."

"Got it in one," Mick said, smiling. "I remember when I was first dating my Pamela. I wouldn't have taken kindly to having to work overtime and not see her because some dopes were beating up on mailboxes.

"Of course, Pam and I have been married for five years now and have two kids and another on the way. So...hey, I'll take a double shift. No problem. Babies are expensive and I could use the overtime money."

"I see," Cable said slowly, still tapping the pencil. "And just who told you that I was seeing Lindsey, Mick?"

"My mother. I stopped by her place on the way in this morning to take her some sweet rolls that Pammy baked. My mom was all excited because Sheriff Montana was seen at Hamilton House last night having dinner with Lindsey Patterson from The Green Thumb nursery. You two are big news in town, Cable."

"Mmm," Cable said, then frowned as the pencil snapped in half from the pressure he was suddenly exerting on it.

"You're royally ticked," Mick said, staring at the pencil.

"No, no, not at all," Cable said, dropping the pieces of the pencil into the trash basket. "I knew word would get around that Lindsey and I were together last night. But by breakfast time this morning? That's setting records even for the buzzing gossip-bees of Prescott."

Mick laughed. "My grandmother telephoned my mother at dawn with the bulletin."

"Unbelievable," Cable said, shaking his head.

"So, anyway," Mick said with a shrug, "none of us are going to complain if you don't want to take a shift looking for the mailbox hoodlums. We'll cover for you, Cable."

"That's very generous of you, Mick, but I'll do my part. I'll start patrolling about ten o'clock tonight. I'll leave it to you, as head deputy, to set up a schedule for the others. Let's get these yo-yos off the streets."

Mick got to his feet. "Well, okay, if you say so, but are you really certain you want a ten-o'clock detail? I mean, ten o'clock is after the news on television and the old romantic late movies come on and—"

''Goodbye, Mick.''

''See ya, Cable,'' Mick said, heading for the door. ''I think I've overstayed my welcome.''

''Yep.''

Cable sighed and leaned back in the chair again, a frown knitting his brows.

He should, he knew, be pleased that the reaction to the charade with Lindsey was proceeding even faster than he'd expected. Word was spreading about the dinner date at Hamilton House like a fire sweeping across a dry desert prairie. Good. That was good. Let the folks talk, keep those telephone lines crackling, meet over back fences, or wherever it was that gossips did the deed. Yes, things were progressing very well.

Then why, Cable thought, staring into space, was he so bummed?

It was probably due to the fact that he was exhausted since he'd only had snatches of sleep the previous night. There he'd been, tossing and turning, unable to erase the image of Lindsey from his mind, unable to shove aside the remembrance of her feminine aroma and the sound of her delightful laughter.

He hadn't been intimate with a woman since his divorce and his body had betrayed him during the very long, dark hours of the night. He'd ached for Lindsey, wanted her with an intensity and need that had finally driven him to take a cold shower in the middle of the night, which hadn't helped one damn bit.

He was so disgusted with himself, Cable fumed, he could spit nails. When he'd taken Lindsey home last night, they hadn't even sat down close together on the sofa. Nope, they'd stood just inside the door in her living room and agreed that the dinner had been delicious and the evening enjoyable.

Yeah, they'd just stood there, and it had taken every ounce of willpower he'd possessed to keep from hauling Lindsey into his arms and kissing her delectable, beckoning lips. He'd finally brushed his thumb over those lips, which had just about been his undoing...then turned and hightailed it out the door.

If he didn't get his act together, he was going to blow this...big time. Everything was falling into place, their plan already accomplishing far more than he'd hoped for this early on.

The only thing *not* under control was him. Well, he had the remainder of the day to get a grip. By the time he went to Lindsey's tonight for dinner, he'd have taken command of his raging needs and would be behaving true to form as the mature adult that he was.

He'd keep his hands in his pockets and off Lindsey Patterson and focus on the ultimate goal of regaining the peace and contentment he'd felt before the matchmakers descended.

Buddy woke from a nap, yawned, then rolled over onto his back on the throw rug where he slept in Cable's office.

"You're awake, huh?" Cable said to the puppy. "Okay, that means a trip outside for you. But don't speak to me, Buddy. Do you know how much it's going to cost to replace the electrical cord to the washing machine?"

Cable got to his feet, scooped up the dog and headed out of his office.

"I'll be right back," Cable said to Mary-Margaret as he passed her desk.

"You should be grateful Buddy didn't get a shock from chewing that cord," Mary-Margaret said. "Count your blessings, Cable."

"I *am* grateful," Cable said, not slowing his steps. "Now I'm into mad as hell at this mutt."

When Cable returned from walking Buddy, the puppy ran ahead of him and made a beeline for underneath Mary-Margaret's desk.

"I'll protect you from this mean man, Buddy," Mary-Margaret said. "That electrical cord was there, tempting you, and you were all alone and what does he expect you to do? Play solitaire? What are you going to do with Buddy tonight, Cable?"

"Tonight?" Cable said, stopping by Mary-Margaret's desk. "Why would you bring up tonight?"

"Well, I assume you'll be seeing Lindsey Patterson this evening," she said, smiling pleasantly. "Heavens, everyone knows that you two enjoyed yourself at Hamilton House last night, so why wouldn't you repeat the performance? It just doesn't make sense that you wouldn't be with Lindsey again tonight. Thus my question of what to do with Buddy while you're away from home." She paused. "Of course, maybe Lindsey is coming over to your place, in which case you wouldn't have to worry about Buddy because you'd both be there to be certain that he didn't get into mischief.

"Then again," she rambled on, "you don't want to be in a position where you have to watch the dog every minute you two are together. After all—"

"That's it," Cable said, raising both hands. "Enough. I'm going out on patrol for a while. I want to check on Aunt Charity, too."

"Good. I haven't heard what kind of night Aunt Charity had. I'll be waiting for your report on her," Mary-Margaret said.

"You don't know if Aunt Charity slept well?" Cable said, raising his eyebrows. "You're slipping,

Mary-Margaret. It's the middle of the afternoon already and you don't have an update on Aunt Charity?''

"My stars, you're grumpy," Mary-Margaret said. "If you're on a rip because folks are buzzing about you and Lindsey Patterson, then you shouldn't have taken her to dinner here in town. You reap what you sow, Sheriff Montana."

Cable chuckled. "That's very profound." He sighed. "No, I'm not upset that everyone is talking about me and Lindsey. I expected as much. It just takes a bit of getting used to, that's all."

"It's not vicious gossip, Cable," Mary-Margaret said. "People care about you and Lindsey. Why should the two of you spend your lives alone if you can discover true love together?"

"All I did was take the woman out for a meal," Cable said, flinging out his arms. "You people have us living happily ever after already."

"We do not," Mary-Margaret said with a little sniff. "But we're certainly going to keep close tabs on the situation to see how it develops."

"I'm outta here," Cable said, shaking his head. He was blowing the program. The matchmakers were behaving right on the mark. "Where's my dog?"

"Leave Buddy with me," Mary-Margaret said. "He's asleep on my foot."

* * *

Lindsey peered into the meat counter at the grocery store, inspecting the T-bone steaks.

"None of those, Lindsey," a man said.

Lindsey's head snapped up to see the butcher standing on the opposite side of the display case.

"What's wrong with them, Jasper?" she said.

"Nothing at all," Jasper said, "except a man the size of Sheriff Montana needs a bigger steak than any of those I've put out. I'll get you a proper-size one from the back. I'll only be a second."

"Wait a minute," Lindsey said. "How did Cable Montana get into this?"

"Well, mercy, Lindsey, it stands to reason that you're going to cook for him tonight, seeing as how he bought you dinner at Hamilton House last evening. That's how you modern, liberated womenfolk do things. Right? Keep it even, equal, and all that." Jasper leaned forward and looked in Lindsey's shopping cart. "Uh-oh."

"Uh-oh?" she echoed. "What? What?"

"You've got fresh broccoli in there. Cable doesn't like broccoli. We were talking about vegetables one time when I saw him in the produce department. Corn. The man is into corn. You're not going to score any points putting trees on his plate, missy."

"Well, I happen to like broccoli," Lindsey said, lifting her chin.

"No harm in that," Jasper said. "You fix trees for yourself and corn for Cable. That's simple enough. Now, do you want that bigger steak or not?"

Lindsey sighed. "Yes, all right. I guess the big news tomorrow morning will be that Sheriff Montana had a huge steak and a mountain of corn at Lindsey Patterson's house this evening."

"What's for dessert?" Jasper said, grinning.

Lindsey narrowed her eyes. "Go get the humongous steak, Jasper."

"Yes, ma'am," Jasper said, laughing. "Whatever you say, Ms. Lindsey."

As Jasper disappeared into the rear, Lindsey wrinkled her nose as she looked at the broccoli in her shopping cart.

So, fine, she'd put the trees back and buy corn, she thought. Only in Prescott would it be known what kind of veggies the eligible bachelors preferred, for crying out loud.

Lindsey sighed and tapped one fingertip on her forehead where a nagging headache had plagued her the entire day.

This headache was caused by fatigue, she knew, because she hadn't slept well. She'd been so restless she'd ended up having to practically remake the bed in the middle of the night, tucking all four corners of the fitted sheet back into place.

Lindsey shifted the tapping fingertip to her lips, resting it there lightly. How was it possible, she mused, that the brush of a man's callused thumb over a woman's lips could be so...so sensual? That gesture of Cable's had been fleeting, but it had been enough to cause heated desire to thrum through her and cause her to toss and turn during the long hours of the night.

This would never do. She had to get a grip on her reaction to Cable or she'd never survive the weeks ahead during the charade.

Or maybe it wouldn't be weeks. The news of their dinner date at Hamilton House was everywhere, just zipping through town. All the customers at The Green Thumb today had made a comment or two on the big event of the previous evening.

Yep, maybe she and Cable could accomplish their goal in far less time than they'd anticipated. That would be good. Wouldn't it? Well, yes, of course, it would. Then again, she'd been looking forward to a break in her routine, some pleasant evenings in the company of an attractive, attentive man. A *safe* escort.

Safe? Oh, ha. Cable Montana was as dangerous as they came. Tall, dark and handsome, oozing sex appeal and blatant masculinity, the sheriff was a walking, talking menace to her state of mind and her wanton body.

Well, no, that wasn't quite fair. Cable was just being himself, wasn't doing one thing to cause her to yell foul while they acted out their roles in the charade. *She* was the one who was out of control. It wasn't Cable's fault that she melted like ice cream in the summer sun when she was in close proximity to him.

Cable had, no doubt, slept like a baby last night, while she was flopping all over her bed. He wasn't having a problem with his part in this nonsense, *she* was.

And enough was enough. She was getting her act together right now. She'd serve Cable a dinner of steak and corn so the busybodies could see his vehicle parked in her driveway. They'd watch a movie on television, then she'd send him packing. She'd go to bed and sleep, having regained command of her wayward thoughts and taken charge of her naughty body and its reaction to Cable Montana.

"Very good," Lindsey said, nodding decisively.

"You haven't even looked at it yet," Jasper said.

"What?" Lindsey turned to see the butcher displaying a huge steak on a piece of white paper.

"Oh, that's fine. Ridiculously large, but fine. Add a small one for me and thank you, Jasper."

"Don't forget the corn," Jasper said. "Say, you haven't heard how Aunt Charity is today, have you?"

"Yes, I called Andrea. Aunt Charity is about the same. No better, no worse. Ben is keeping very close tabs on her because he's concerned about that nasty cold going into pneumonia."

"Mmm," Jasper said, nodding. "I'll get this steak wrapped and weighed for you, Lindsey." He paused. "You never did tell me what you planned to have for dessert tonight."

"Gosh, Jasper," she said, batting her eyelashes. "Do you think I should offer coffee, tea…or me?"

A flush crept up Jasper's neck and onto his cheeks. "I was going to suggest chocolate chip cookies."

Lindsey stood in front of the full-length mirror on the back of her bedroom door and cocked her head from one side to the other as she scrutinized her appearance.

Jeans, a red string sweater and tennis shoes. This outfit was definitely not big-city chic. But, hey, she didn't live in a big city. Besides, she was going to barbecue the steaks in the backyard, for Pete's sake. And furthermore, she wasn't supposed to be attempting to impress Cable.

"Ah, vanity," she said to her reflection, "thy name is woman. Do I care whether Cable thinks I look nice? No. Yes. No." She spun around and marched toward the bedroom door. "Forget it. I'm driving myself nuts."

As Lindsey entered the living room, a knock sounded at the front door, and her heart did a funny little tap dance that caused her to roll her eyes in self-disgust. She crossed the room and opened the door.

"Hello, Cable," she said, smiling. "Oh, gosh, am I under arrest?"

Cable stepped into the living room and Lindsey closed the door behind him.

"I have to go on patrol later," he said, "so I'm stuck wearing the uniform all evening. I figured bringing a change of clothes was a bit more fuel for the gossip mill than we cared to supply."

Lindsey laughed. "No joke. This whole thing is already set on high-speed. It's amazing." She paused and frowned. "It's also a bit...oh, I don't know...unsettling."

"I know what you mean," Cable said, nodding. "It definitely requires some getting used to. We'll probably learn to take it all in stride about the time we don't need to act out this charade anymore. This togetherness of ours will all be over soon.''

''Yes, I suppose it will,'' Lindsey said quietly, looking into Cable's green eyes. ''Over. Soon.''

They stood there, hardly breathing, gazes holding, as heated desire began to thrum and swirl and coil within them. Cable raised one hand as though to reach out and touch Lindsey, then blinked as he saw his hand appear in his hazy vision. He snapped his hand back to his side and cleared his throat.

''I like your sweater,'' he said, hearing the strange rasp of his voice. ''Red is a great color on you.''

''Your uniform is sensational on you, too,'' Lindsey said rather dreamily. Her eyes widened in horror in the next instant. ''What I mean is…never mind. Let's go outside, shall we? I'm going to barbecue for us. Yes, that's what I'm going to do, all right. Barbecue steaks and serve them with salad and corn. Not broccoli, perish the thought. Nope, it's corn. Good old corn and…'' She sighed. ''I'm babbling like an idiot.''

''Lindsey,'' Cable said, ''I think we need to talk. Let's sit down for a minute. Okay?''

Lindsey nodded and they settled onto the sofa a cushion apart. They shifted slightly so they could look directly at each other.

''How did you sleep last night?'' Cable said.

"You want to have an in-depth discussion about how I slept?" Lindsey said.

"Just answer the question," Cable said. "In all fairness, I'll go first. I didn't sleep worth a damn. Why? Because I wanted you, Lindsey Patterson. I was tied in knots with wanting you and I couldn't sleep."

"No kidding?" she said, smiling brightly. She sobered in the next second. "I mean, oh...really? My, my, that's a shame, Cable. You must be exhausted, and I didn't sleep well, either, because I kept thinking about what it might be like to make love with you and I tossed and turned and...I really can't believe I'm telling you this."

"Hey," he said, moving close to her. "We're being mature adults here. Honest and open."

"Honest?" she said, her voice rising. "You call acting out a charade for the benefit of a town being honest?"

"No, but we're being honest with each other. We're healthy, normal people who...I'm not proposing that we...I'm just saying that we're aware of the attraction between us and..." Cable's voice trailed off and he frowned.

"And?" Lindsey prompted.

"Hell, I don't know," he said. "We can agree to ignore the...the...or we can agree to..." He shook his head. "I've never taken part in a conversation like this before in my life. Look, we can sleep together or not. It's up to us. There.''

''Oh, that was so-o-o tacky,'' Lindsey said, getting to her feet.

Cable stood. ''Well, how would you get it out on the table? Damn it, Lindsey, the attraction between us is practically crackling through the air. We have to decide what we're going to do about it. I sure as hell didn't plan on it, but it happened.''

''I know,'' she said, wrapping her hands around her elbows. ''But I just can't be so clinical about this, making the choice like choosing between broccoli and corn.''

''Yeah, you're right,'' Cable said wearily. ''This discussion is definitely leaning toward tacky.'' He paused. ''How's this? We'll just do whatever seems right...for both of us...whenever it seems right...if it does. Hell. I used to be able to speak like I had a brain.''

''No, no, what you said is fine,'' Lindsey said. ''I understood what you meant. We're adults, and we can do what feels natural and right and real, or come to the conclusion that it wouldn't be natural and right and real, in which case we wouldn't...I'm going to go start the grill outside now.''

Before Lindsey could move, Cable gripped her shoulders, keeping her in place.

"We should do what feels natural and right and real?" he said.

"Well, yes," Lindsey said, nodding. "Don't you think that makes sense?"

"Oh, yes, Ms. Patterson," Cable said, "I most certainly do."

And then he lowered his head and kissed her.

## Chapter Six

This kiss, Lindsey thought, as her lashes drifted down, was so natural and so very, very right. And real? If it became any more *real*, she was going to dissolve into a heap at Cable's feet.

Lindsey's arms floated upward to encircle Cable's neck, and he nestled her to his aroused body as he wrapped his arms around her. He raised his head for a fraction of a second to draw a rough breath, slanted his mouth in the opposite direction and claimed Lindsey's lips once again.

Natural? Right? Real? Cable thought hazily. Oh, yeah, these kisses were all that, and more. And

Lindsey? She was responding to him totally, giving of herself, holding nothing back. She wanted him as much as he wanted her.

Lindsey stiffened and broke the kiss.

"What..." he started.

"Your badge," Lindsey said, then eased out of Cable's embrace. "It was poking me."

"Oh. I'm sorry. I'll take it off and—"

"No, no," Lindsey said, wrapping her hands around her elbows. She drew a wobbly breath, then met Cable's gaze. "That won't be necessary, because we're not going to...I don't think we should have...darn it, Cable, what on earth are we doing?"

"What feels natural and right and real," he said. "There was nothing wrong with what just happened here, Lindsey, what we shared. We desire each other, want each other. You can't deny that."

"No, I can't, but it doesn't mean we should..." Lindsey shook her head. "This is all so confusing. It's happening too quickly, too. I don't know, Cable. We're playing out a charade. Where does the script for our performance end and the *real* begin?"

"Those kisses were real," he said, his voice rising. "What happens between us when we shut the door is ours, has nothing to do with the busybodies in town. Do you understand what I'm saying to you?''

Lindsey planted her hands on her hips. ''I understand that you're yelling your head off at me.''

''I apologize for hollering,'' he said, dragging a hand through his hair, ''but it's important that you believe me when I say that I kissed you because I wanted to, needed to, not because of any role I'm playing. Do you, Lindsey? Believe that?''

Lindsey looked directly into Cable's eyes for a long moment, then nodded. ''Yes,'' she said softly, ''I do.''

''Good. That's good.''

''But it's complicating what should have been so simple,'' she said, throwing out her hands. ''Enough of this. How would you like the biggest steak in the history of steaks for your dinner? And—'' she pointed one finger in the air ''—I have corn. Oodles of corn. Let it not be said that I attempted to serve broccoli to the sheriff of Prescott.''

''Heaven forbid, ma'am,'' Cable said, encircling Lindsey's shoulders with one arm. ''I can't abide those green, wiggly tree things. Lead me to this steak, Ms. Patterson. I'm a starving man.''

The dinner was delicious and to Lindsey's wide-eyed amazement Cable devoured every bite of the enormous steak. They ate at a small table on Lindsey's patio in the backyard, enjoying the cool summer breeze. After the dishes had been cleared away, they stayed outside, settling onto lounge chairs that were set side by side.

Lindsey had turned off the kitchen light and they sat in the glow of the silvery moon and the multitude of stars that twinkled in the heavens.

"I may not move for a week," Cable said, then patted his flat stomach. "That was a delicious dinner, Lindsey. Thank you very much."

"You're welcome," she said, staring up at the gorgeous sky. "You have Jasper the butcher to thank for that steak. He picked it out especially for you. He also saved you from the broccoli trees." She laughed softly. "This town is unbelievable."

"There are good people here. They care about each other, they really do." Cable paused. "I guess Aunt Charity isn't showing any improvement yet."

"No, she's not," Lindsey said, frowning. "She stayed in bed all day again, which is an indication that she's really feeling badly. It takes an awful lot to slow Aunt Charity down."

"Well, she has the best of care," Cable said. "Ben is a top-notch doctor."

"That's true." Lindsey sighed. "Mmm. I'm so full, so mellow. Don't take it personally if I doze." Oh, what a joke. She was so incredibly *aware* of

Cable, of him being just inches away, and the memories of those kisses shared were tormenting her, causing her to want more, want him. "Just poke me if I fall asleep."

"I might nod off myself," Cable said. "I am very comfortable sitting here." Wrong. He was battling the urge to scoop Lindsey into his arms and nestle her on top of him in the lounge chair. There was a coil of heat tightening low in his body and— "That would cause a stir, wouldn't it? If my vehicle was in your driveway all night because we fell asleep out here?"

"Don't even think about it. The town would go nuts." Lindsey turned her head to look at Cable. "What did you do with Buddy tonight? You said during dinner that he ate the washing machine cord, but you didn't mention what new plan of action you took."

"It's foolproof," Cable said. "I went to a used furniture store and bought one of those mesh baby playpens. I put newspaper in it, Buddy's water and food, his toys, the whole bit. He's in his neat little house in the middle of the living room. There's no way he can get into any trouble in that playpen."

Lindsey laughed. "That's what you said about the laundry room."

"I know," Cable said, frowning. "But I out-smarted him this time." He glanced at his watch.

"Well, hell, I've got to hit the road. We're trying to nab those guys who are smashing people's mailboxes and we're doubling up on shifts to do it. I really hate to leave, Lindsey. This has been a fantastic evening."

"I enjoyed it, too," she said.

Cable got to his feet and extended one hand to assist Lindsey out of the chair. He drew her up but didn't release her hand as he looked at her questioningly.

"Your call," he said quietly. "I'm not going to pressure you. I don't want you to be uneasy when you're with me. I'd like to kiss you good-night, but I won't if you don't want me to. As I said, your call."

Should she? Or shouldn't she? Lindsey thought. Oh, forget it. She was wearing out her brain. She was going to do what felt natural and right and real in the moment at hand.

Lindsey pulled her hand free of Cable's gentle grasp, raised on tiptoe to entwine her arms around his neck and kissed him.

Cable stiffened for an instant in surprise, then in the next heartbeat encircled Lindsey with his arms and molded her slender body against him. He parted her lips and delved his tongue into her mouth, finding her tongue, stroking, dueling, as passions soared.

Yes, Lindsey thought. Oh, Cable.

Lindsey, Lindsey, Cable's mind hammered. He was going up in smoke and flames, burning with the heat of his desire for this woman. He had never, *never,* wanted anyone the way he did her. This was so damn right and so damn real and so—

"Oh, ow," Lindsey said, jerking backward. "That badge is turning me into a pincushion."

"Hell," Cable said, as Lindsey stepped out of his embrace. "That does it. I resign. I'm no longer the sheriff and the badge is off the shirt. I'll get a job sweeping floors at Hamilton House or something, but my days of being a badge-wearing, gun-toting lawman are over."

Lindsey laughed in delight at Cable's outrageous outburst, then framed his face in her hands and gave him a quick peck on the lips.

"You are so funny," she said, smiling at him warmly, "and you make me laugh right out loud, and I like you, Cable Montana. I really do."

"Oh," Cable said, then nodded. "That's nice, a special compliment and I appreciate it. I like you, too, Lindsey Patterson, as a person, a woman. Yep, I do, and that's important.

"Whatever we decide to do, we can be assured that there's a foundation of friendship, of liking and respecting each other. That's a rather new concept for me, but it's good, I think. Yes, it definitely is.''

"I agree." Lindsey smiled and patted the badge on Cable's shirt. "Go catch the bad guys, Sheriff. How are people going to pay their bills if they don't have a mailbox so the bills can be put into it and they can take them out and pay them?" She laughed. "A person can't go through life without a mailbox, for mercy's sake."

"'Tis true. Walk me to the door so that you lock up behind me."

They went through the house to the front door.

"Are you going to stop by your place and get Buddy so he can go on patrol with you?" Lindsey said.

"There's a thought. Yes, I think I will. It will be a reward for him for being cooped up in the playpen and unable to destroy anything. I don't want to mess up his little psyche by having him spend too many hours not getting into trouble."

Lindsey laughed again, then sighed in contentment. "Thank you for a very special evening, Cable," she said. "I enjoyed every minute of it."

"Ditto." He dropped a quick kiss on her lips. "I'll talk to you tomorrow and we'll decide what our next outing together should be."

"All right."

Cable left the house and Lindsey closed and

locked the door. She turned and leaned against it, a soft smile on her lips.

She had really had a...well, a wonderful time with Cable tonight, she mused. She liked being with him and also liked how she felt about herself when they were together.

And the kisses? Heavenly days, she'd never experienced such instant, raging desire, such thrumming heat within her, such—

She wanted to make love with Cable Montana and there was no doubt in her mind that he wanted her, too.

Could she do it? Engage in a no-strings, no-commitment affair?

Just how emotionally dangerous would that be? What if she lost her heart to Cable, actually blew the whole charade and fell in love with the man? That would be terrible, just devastating.

She could not, would not, fall in love with anyone, not ever again. To be in love would lead to wanting it all—a husband, babies, a home filled with love and laughter, and none of those things were hers to have.

She knew that.

It was etched in stone in her heart, mind and soul, and had been for three very long years.

"No, no." Lindsey waved her hands in the air

and started across the room. "Don't think it to death."

She stopped in the middle of the room and stared at the far wall where an entertainment center held her television set, VCR, stereo and a multitude of books.

In her mind's eye she envisioned a fireplace there with warm, leaping flames and the golden circle of light they created. She saw Cable reach for her as they sat on the floor in front of the hearth and she moved into his arms eagerly, anticipating the moment when they would—

"Gracious," Lindsey said, patting her cheeks, which were suddenly flushed with heat. "Enough of this, you wanton woman."

She didn't have a crystal ball, she thought, as she began to close up the house for the night. She had no idea what might transpire between her and Cable. But there was one thing she did know for certain—she and Cable might be putting on a phony show for the matchmakers while out in public, but once they were alone behind closed doors, what happened between them must be natural and right and real.

And she knew, just somehow knew, that whatever transpired with Cable would be just that— natural and right and real. If they chose to make love, well, so be it. She was really in no danger of losing her heart to the man because she had three years of practice at keeping her heart safely protected behind a strong, unbreachable wall.

She was in control, doing fine, Lindsey thought decisively as she headed for bed. She'd just take things as they came, one day, one night at a time. With Cable.

After leaving Lindsey's, Cable stopped at his house. He left the motor running on the Land Rover and sprinted across the yard with the intention of releasing Buddy from his playpen prison and taking the puppy along on patrol.

He let himself in the front door and Buddy bounded across the room with his tail wagging, yipping loudly as he greeted his master. Cable's eyes widened as he swept his gaze over the living room.

There was a jagged hole in the mesh of the playpen large enough for a wiggling Buddy to have escaped from the enclosure. A newspaper had been shredded and strewn across the room, along with a small feather-filled throw pillow that had been on the sofa.

"You trashed the place," Cable said incredulously, staring down at Buddy, who rolled onto his back and thumped the floor with his tail. "You killed the playpen. Demolished the living room.

You're a threat to society and my sanity. What am I going to do with you?''

An I'm-so-excited-to-see-you Buddy bounced to his feet and tinkled on Cable's boot.

Late the next afternoon, Lindsey stood in Cable's backyard and nodded in satisfaction. The enclosures she'd ordered to protect Cable's landscaping from Buddy had arrived at the nursery and she'd spent the afternoon putting them firmly in place.

"That ought to do it," she said, sweeping her gaze over the project.

She pulled off her gardening gloves and started across the yard just as Cable came through the gate.

"Hi," she said, an instant smile on her face. "You have excellent timing. You can see the finished product in all its splendor."

Cable nodded and set Buddy down on the grass. The puppy bounded forward and began to jump straight up in the air near Lindsey.

"You're a furry pogo stick, Buddy," she said, smiling. "Look how high he can go, Cable." She looked at Cable and frowned as she saw his serious expression. "What's wrong? I thought you'd be feeling chipper today because you nabbed the mailbox smashers last night. The word is that they were two sixteen-year-old boys who have been grounded by their parents for eternity.''

"Yeah, we got them,'' Cable said. "They're going to do yard work for the rest of the summer at every house where they destroyed a mailbox. Their parents are holding their driver's licenses for ransom at this point.'' He paused. "Lindsey, I went by the nursery to see you and Glenna-Sue said you were over here so I came right away.''

Lindsey closed the distance between them and looked up at Cable questioningly.

"Why?'' she said. "I mean, you haven't smiled once since you came into the yard. What's wrong?''

"Ben just admitted Aunt Charity to the hospital because she has pneumonia. I'm going over there now. Do you want to come with me?''

"Oh, Cable,'' Lindsey said, feeling the color drain from her face. "What is Ben saying? How serious is this?''

"I don't know. Mary-Margaret called me on the radio in my vehicle with the news. I don't have any details. I told her to contact me on my pager if she needed me, because I was going to be in the hospital finding out what the situation is. I thought you'd want to know and maybe go with me to check things out.''

"Yes. Yes, of course I do,'' Lindsey said, her

voice trembling. "Thank you so much for coming to get me."

"You were the first person I thought of when I got the word from Mary-Margaret," Cable said. "I know you're very fond of Aunt Charity, just as I am, so I set out to find you."

"That's lovely, Cable. So kind and considerate and...I really do thank you so very much."

"Sure. Let's go," he said. "Buddy can stay in the yard now that you've got the bushes and other stuff protected. I don't know, though. He ate the playpen so...never mind. I'll worry about it later." He took off his Stetson, raked a hand through his hair, then settled the hat back on his head, pulling it down low on his forehead. "Come on. We're wasting time standing here."

Lindsey nodded and they hurried from the yard, leaving a wailing Buddy behind the closed gate.

The hospital waiting room on the floor where Aunt Charity was being cared for was packed with people who were speaking in hushed tones.

Charity's twin sister, Prudence, was sitting on one of the sofas, her hands clutched tightly in her lap. She was wearing a plain high-necked, long-sleeve gray dress and her face was pale, accentuating the purple smudges beneath her eyes. Brandon's wife, Andrea, was sitting next to Prudence, speaking quietly to the older woman.

Cable maneuvered his way through the group with Lindsey right behind him. He stopped by Brandon, who was talking to Ben's wife, Megan.

"Brandon?" Cable said. "Hello, Megan. Sorry to interrupt, but could you bring Lindsey and me up-to-date on Aunt Charity's condition?"

Megan smiled. "Hello, Lindsey, Cable. It's nice to see you, but I wish it was under different circumstances."

"No joke," Cable said, nodding. "What's the latest word here?"

"We haven't seen Ben yet," Brandon said. "He's still getting Aunt Charity settled in, I guess. I'm worried about Aunt Prudence, too. She's been so concerned about Charity that she hasn't been sleeping well and she's exhausted. Look at her. She's out on her feet. That's not good for her at her age and..."

Brandon stopped speaking and shook his head.

"This is a nightmare," he said, dragging both hands down his face. "It's strange, you know. I've just gone along thinking that my great-aunts are indestructible, will always be there, living in their apartment in Hamilton House. Aunt Charity would keep giving me hell about everything, and Aunt Prudence would keep the peace and...damn."

"Oh, Brandon," Lindsey said, "you've done what all of us do. I didn't dwell on how elderly my parents were, how frail they were becoming, then—no, we're all being too gloomy. Let's not do this."

"You're right, Lindsey," Megan said, slipping her arm through Brandon's. "Aunt Charity would be furious if she knew we were all getting terribly upset. We've got to calm down and wait until Ben comes and tells us what we need to know."

"There you go." Cable nodded and glanced around. "If Aunt Charity was in this waiting room with all these people, she'd have a game of gin rummy going, penny a point, and she'd have cleaned some clocks."

Brandon laughed. "Ain't that the truth. I've been trying for years to figure out if she cheats at gin rummy, but I don't see how she's doing it if she is. She is so lucky at cards it's a sin."

Aunt Prudence appeared suddenly and smiled up at Brandon.

"It's good to hear laughter in this room, dear," she said. "Charity would like that. Hello, Lindsey, Cable, how nice of you to come."

"It's where we want to be." Cable leaned down and kissed Aunt Prudence on the cheek. "How are you doing, Aunt Prudence?"

"I'm a tiny bit exasperated with myself," she

said, sighing. "Charity and I have talked about the fact that we're getting up in years and can't expect to continue to enjoy our excellent health forever. I'm just having a difficult time realizing that this has happened to Charity, I guess. I must behave like the mature woman I supposedly am. But, oh, children, Charity is so ill and..." Prudence stopped speaking as tears filled her eyes.

"Hey, now," Cable said, wrapping one arm around Prudence's shoulders. "You go right ahead and cry if you feel like it. There's no shame in that." He reached into his back pocket, then pressed a pristine white handkerchief into Prudence's hands. "Here."

"Thank you, dear," Prudence said, dabbing at her nose. "No, I won't cry. Brandon's laughter was like music and I'm not going to drown that lovely sound with weeping. I do wish that Ben would tell us how Charity is doing, though."

"Is this where the gin rummy game is being held?" a voice said from the doorway.

Everyone turned as Ben entered the room. He spotted Aunt Prudence and came to where she stood, kissing her on the cheek when he arrived, then giving Megan a quick kiss.

"Well, folks," Ben said, loud enough for everyone to hear, "we've got Aunt Charity settled in and as comfortable as possible. She has viral pneumonia so there isn't a lot we can do to fight it. She's on oxygen to help her breathe more easily. That's all I can tell you really. What we do now is wait.''

"May I sit with her, dear?" Aunt Prudence said.

"No, Aunt Prudence, you can't," Ben said. "Not now. Andrea and Brandon are going to take you home and you're going to get some rest. That's not a suggestion, that's doctor's orders, and I'm the doctor."

"Oh, but—" Prudence started.

"No arguments," Ben said. "Andrea, Brandon, you have your assignment. Aunt Pru, you can come back later after you've had a good nap. If there's any change in Charity's condition, I'll call you immediately."

Prudence sighed, nodded, then allowed herself to be led from the room by Andrea and Brandon. The remainder of the well-wishers wandered out, telling Ben they'd be calling the hospital for updates. Megan kissed Ben goodbye and said she'd go home and start dinner.

"I've got to get back to my office and finish seeing today's patients," Ben said to Lindsey and Cable. "You two are the only ones left here. You might as well shove off for now."

"I'd like to stay for a while," Lindsey said. "I

know I can't do anything to help, but I'd just feel better being here for a bit.''

"That's fine," Ben said. "I'll tell the nurse on duty to keep you informed.''

"Thank you, Ben," Lindsey said, then looked at Cable. "I know I rode with you, Cable, but I can walk home later, or telephone for a taxi.''

Cable frowned. "I'm not going anywhere. Mary-Margaret knows that she can reach me on my pager. Do you think I'd leave you alone in this room to worry and stew, Lindsey? Not a chance. If you're staying, then so am I.''

"That's very nice of you, Cable," Lindsey said, smiling at him warmly.

Their eyes met and Cable matched Lindsey's warm smile. Neither one of them noticed when a chuckling Ben Rizzoli left the room.

## Chapter Seven

Lindsey went in search of a telephone to call The Green Thumb and tell Glenna-Sue to close up at the regular time. She had, she told Cable, two part-time employees who were students at Yavapai College, so everything was under control at the nursery.

Cable went downstairs to the cafeteria and returned with wrapped sandwiches and soft drinks for their dinner. They ate the makeshift meal, then settled back on the rather lumpy sofa.

"I realize there's no point in us sitting here," Lindsey said. "We would get word if there was any change in Aunt Charity's condition, but I don't know, I just feel I want to be as close to her as possible for now."

"You really love her, don't you?" Cable said.

"Yes. Yes, I do," Lindsey said, staring at her hands clutched in her lap. "And I love Aunt Prudence, too.

"When I first arrived in town and was putting in horrendously long days getting The Green Thumb ready to open, the aunts suddenly appeared at the nursery one day. They had come in a taxi, and scooped me up and took me to lunch. I was so exhausted I was punchy and they said, as my self-appointed aunties, they'd decided I needed a break and a hot meal.

"That was how I met them. They'd heard I was new in town, surmised that I was working too hard and set out to be certain that I didn't feel so alone. I've never forgotten their kindness. It meant so much to me. I burst into tears right in the middle of lunch because I was so tired and they were so wonderful, so caring."

Cable nodded. "That sounds like the aunts. They're very special ladies." He chuckled. "I bet they were in on the matchmaking you endured when your turn came up."

"Oh, yes, indeed they were," Lindsey said, smiling. "When I was finally declared a hopeless case, Aunt Charity said she'd like to paddle my bottom for being so set in my ways. She said that I'd be a marvelous wife and mother and what in the…to quote…devil's brew…was the matter with me to be so stubborn about not getting married?''

''Well,'' Cable said, running his hand over his chin, ''Aunt Charity has a valid point. I think you *would* be a fantastic wife and mother, Lindsey.

''I remember that you said you value your independence and that the nursery takes up a great deal of your time, but the more I get to know you the harder it is to envision you living out your days alone. It just doesn't…doesn't fit who you are.''

A cold fist tightened in Lindsey's stomach and she got to her feet.

*It's not who I am,* she thought, as she began to pace around the room. She wanted to be a wife, to be married to a man she loved beyond reason and who returned that love in kind. And, oh, how she yearned to be the mother of a child created with that man.

She shouldn't have rambled on about what Aunt Charity had said regarding the subject. She was upset about Aunt Charity being so ill, was emotionally vulnerable.

Dear heaven, she was a breath away from crying, and if she didn't get it together, she might blurt out the truth to Cable about why she could not, would not, ever get married. No, no, no, that mustn't happen.

"Marriage and motherhood just aren't for everyone," she said breezily, stopping her trek to look at a spot on the wall above Cable's head. "And that, as they say, is the end of the story."

Cable narrowed his eyes and studied Lindsey intently. It didn't even take his years of being a cop to realize that something wasn't right here, that Lindsey wasn't telling the truth.

Lindsey was obviously making a point of not meeting his gaze, and her voice was trembling slightly and—no, this wasn't the end of the story as she said. Lindsey Patterson was hiding something.

Now what secret was lovely Lindsey hiding from him?

Even more, would she ever come to trust him enough to confide in him what that secret deep within her was?

Why was that suddenly so important...Lindsey trusting him to that degree? Hell, he didn't know why it mattered so much to him, but it did. It really did.

"Cable," Lindsey said, "why are you staring at me as if I have a bug on my nose?"

"What? Oh, sorry, I was just woolgathering." Cable frowned. "Did you ever stop and think about that word? *Woolgathering.* Weird. Why not just say *daydreaming,* which makes sense when you hear it.''

Lindsey shrugged. ''I don't know. I think *woolgathering* is collecting data. *Daydreaming* is more like wishful thinking. I could be completely wrong, of course, but that's how I've always distinguished between the two.'' She sat back down next to Cable.

''Do you daydream?'' he said quietly.

''Not often,'' she said, turning her head to meet his gaze. ''If a person gets carried away with fantasizing, they're setting themselves up to be blue when they realize none of those daydreams will come true. Woolgathering, by my definition, is more practical and realistic.''

''Mmm,'' Cable said, nodding. ''Tell me one of your daydreams.''

Lindsey frowned. ''Why?''

''Why not?'' he said, raising his eyebrows. ''We're just filling the time while we're sitting here. You tell me one of your daydreams, and I'll share one of mine with you. How's that?''

''I...I don't want to play this game, Cable,'' Lindsey said, shifting her gaze to her hands, clutched in her lap again.

''Don't you trust me enough to share your dreams with me, Lindsey?''

Lindsey's head snapped up and she looked directly into Cable's eyes.

"It has nothing to do with trust," she said. "It's like I said before—daydreams can be damaging to a person's peace of mind, their happiness. Daydreams are what you want and…and will never have and…Cable, please, enough of this. Let's change the subject."

"Hey," he said, covering her hands with one of his, "I'm sorry. I didn't mean to upset you."

"No, I'm the one who is sorry. I'm overreacting to everything because I'm so worried about Aunt Charity. I'm really super in a crisis, aren't I? I'm falling apart."

Cable gave Lindsey's hands a quick squeeze, then got to his feet.

"I'll go talk to the nurse on duty and see if I can get any kind of an update on Aunt Charity's condition," he said. "Okay?"

"Thank you, Cable," she said, managing to produce a small smile. "Again, you're being so considerate and…well, I truly thank you for being so patient with me."

"It's no great effort on my part," he said, frowning. "I care about you, Lindsey. I…well, I truly do."

"I care about you, too, Cable," she said softly. "You're a very special man."

Their gazes met and held as Cable stood towering above Lindsey.

Her breath caught as she felt the now familiar heat of desire begin to thrum and swirl within her. Her heart began to beat in a wild tempo and the room seemed to disappear into a mist, leaving only Cable within her view. She couldn't think. She could hardly breathe. She could only want and need Cable Montana.

"No," she said, tearing her gaze from his.

Cable hunkered down in front of her and placed one hand on one of her knees.

"You're turning me inside out, Lindsey Patterson," he said, his voice raspy. "You truly are. Right now, in this room, is not the time to address this, but it isn't going to go away. We're going to have to decide, together, what is natural and right and real. You want me. I want you. What are we going to do about it?"

Lindsey lifted her chin. "Does the solution come under woolgathering or daydreaming, Cable? Do you intend to gather facts to reach a conclusion? Or will the answer come from fantasizing? Is this all very clinical, or is it romantic and important and…oh, never mind."

Cable planted his hands on his thighs and pushed himself to his feet.

"If we make love, Lindsey," he said, an edge

of anger to his voice, "it will be very special and very important and very meaningful. Don't you know that?"

Lindsey sighed. "Yes. Yes, I know that. What I said was uncalled for, and I'm sorry." She pressed her hands to her cheeks. "I'm behaving so badly. Ignore me. Pretend I'm not here."

Yeah, right, Cable thought dryly. He couldn't *ignore* Lindsey Patterson when he wasn't even with her, let alone when he was inches away from her.

Pretend she wasn't here? Hell, she'd taken up permanent residency in his brain. And his body? He'd better not dwell on that part of his being, or he might very well haul Lindsey to her feet, kiss her senseless, then—

Cable cleared his throat, spun around and started toward the doorway to the waiting room.

"I'll go talk to the nurse on duty," he said.

"Will I do?" Ben said, entering the room.

"Ben," Lindsey said, getting to her feet. "Why are you back here so soon? Is Aunt Charity—"

"Whoa," Ben said, raising both hands. "It's been two hours since I left and Megan and I are both here. We met Andrea, Brandon and Aunt Prudence in the lobby, and they're all in saying hello to Aunt Charity right now. I gave them five minutes because Charity is very tired and needs her rest.''

''Is she any better at all?'' Lindsey said, wrapping her hands around her elbows.

''Her temperature is down one full degree,'' Ben said. ''Hey, I'll take anything I can get at this point. I definitely want that temperature down a lot more in the next twenty-four hours, but we'll have to wait and see. Charity was threatening to tan my hide if I didn't let her have company, so you two are up next for five minutes, if you want to see her.''

''Oh, yes, thank you, Ben,'' Lindsey said. ''I promise not to stay one second longer than five minutes.''

''Okay, come with me,'' Ben said. ''I'll toss the others out, then you guys can go in.''

''How's Aunt Prudence doing?'' Cable said.

''She looks a lot better,'' Ben said. ''She had a nap and some dinner. Andrea and Brandon are trying to convince her to go home with them, but I doubt they'll win that battle. The aunts are very independent ladies, you know.''

''There's a lot of that going around,'' Cable said, sliding a glance at Lindsey.

''Mmm,'' Lindsey said, glaring at Cable. ''Ben, did Andrea and Brandon bring the baby?''

''No,'' he said, ''the rules don't allow little kids

on the floor to visit. I caught hell from Charity about that, too. She wants to see Ashley right now, thank you very much, but Andrea and Brandon left the baby at a neighbor's.''

''Don't you think the fact that Charity is complaining is a good sign?'' Cable said. ''I mean, she sounds like she's being her usual feisty self.''

''Yes, it points in her favor,'' Ben said, then frowned. ''But she's very ill, Cable. Sometimes, well, sometimes being a feisty fighter just isn't enough to...I just don't know yet what her prognosis is. I just don't.''

''Dear heaven,'' Lindsey whispered.

''Let's go,'' Ben said. ''No gloomy faces in that room, remember.'' He smiled. ''You'd better go in there like sunshine itself, or the patient will give you what-for...guaranteed.''

The trio left the waiting room and met the others outside Charity's room. Greetings and hugs were exchanged, then Lindsey and Cable stepped into the dimly lit private room and moved to the edge of the bed.

Oh, God, Lindsey thought, struggling against threatening tears. Aunt Charity looked so small in that bed, so pale, so...so old and...the oxygen tubes in her nose must be uncomfortable and...she hated this. She really, really hated this.

"I swear, Aunt Charity," Cable said, "what some people won't do to get attention."

"Got you here fussing over me, didn't I, big boy?" Aunt Charity said, her voice sounding thin and weak. "I'm the hit of the show, in the center ring of the circus."

Cable smiled. "Yep, the spotlight is on you big time. Nice work."

"You betcha," Aunt Charity said. "Lindsey, if you cry like you look as though you're planning on doing, I'll send you to your room."

"I promise I won't cry," Lindsey said, blinking away her tears. "Are you in any pain, Aunt Charity?"

"Not much. Feel as though there's a moose sitting on my chest, but this oxygen they're piping into me helps that some." Aunt Charity paused. "You two look good together. Word around town is that you're an item, but I think you've got some shenanigans in the works to keep the matchmakers pleased as punch with themselves."

"Oh, well, um, Cable and I are...um..." Lindsey said, scrambling for a reply to Charity's accusations.

"Give it up, miss," Charity said. "I wasn't born yesterday, you know. Thing is, monkey business has a way of backfiring. You two are feeling very smug with the performance you're putting on for the busybodies, but you just might be surprised at the outcome when the final curtain comes down.''

''What do you mean?'' Lindsey said.

''Speaking of final curtains,'' Ben said, entering the room and walking to the side of the bed. ''This visiting hour is over.''

''Nope,'' Aunt Charity said. ''The fat lady didn't sing, hotshot. I want to talk to these kiddies some more.''

''Tomorrow,'' Ben said. ''You're finished holding court for tonight. Lindsey, Cable, say goodbye to the worst patient in the hospital and hit the road.''

Lindsey and Cable each kissed Aunt Charity on the cheek, bid her good-night, then looked intently at Ben, who nodded, understanding that they wanted to be notified if there was any change in Aunt Charity's condition.

''We'll see you tomorrow,'' Lindsey said from the doorway. ''Sleep well, Aunt Charity.''

''Remember what I said, Lindsey,'' Charity said. ''You, too, Montana. You two are due to get your comeuppance, mark my words.''

''Don't utter another one of your profound words, madam,'' Ben said. ''Go to sleep. Lindsey, Cable, you're gone. See ya.''

Lindsey and Cable left the room and the door closed with a hush.

"Ben, you're a dud," Aunt Charity said. "I have no idea how that darling Megan puts up with you." She paused. "And you need a haircut. You'd better not let me croak, hot stuff, because I've got people, family, to look after in this town."

"I know you do, sweet lady," Ben said, bending over to kiss her on the forehead.

"Ben," Charity said, taking one of his hands in one of hers, "if I do get beat out by this nasty bug, you watch over Prudence. Everyone will need to watch over Prudence." She sighed and closed her eyes. "Nope, forget that. I can't check out yet. Want…to go…to the wedding. I do…fancy attending…pretty…weddings."

"What wedding?" Ben said, but Aunt Charity was sound asleep.

Ben checked the IV hanging on the pole next to the bed, smoothed Aunt Charity's blanket, looked at her for a long, worried moment, then left the room.

Charity stirred. "I'll get…new…dress…for the wedding. She'll be a…beautiful…bride, and that hunk…of stuff…will be a…handsome groom. And that…will be the last…of the Bachelor Bet. Everyone will be matched up…and happy. Right, Ben? You bet. Lindsey and Cable…will be…perfect…together."

Sleep claimed Aunt Charity once again and she

quieted. The only sound in the room was her labored breathing.

As Cable drove out of the hospital parking lot, Lindsey shifted in her seat to face him as much as her seat belt would allow.

"Cable," she said, a rather frantic edge to her voice, "Aunt Charity knows. Did you hear her? She has figured out that we're putting on a charade for the matchmakers. I don't believe this. How did she do that? Know exactly what we're doing?"

"Beats me," Cable said, lifting one shoulder in a shrug. "I guess she has a sixth sense, or wisdom of age, or some such thing."

"She'll blow the whistle on us, I just know she will. Oh, this is terrible." Lindsey sank back against the seat. "Listen to me. I'm going on and on about our problem when we're not even certain that Aunt Charity will be able to fight the pneumonia, and I don't want to think about that. But she looked so small and frail in that bed, so pale."

Cable chuckled. "She had plenty to say, though. Even as ill as she is, she's still keeping everyone in line."

"She said we would get our comeuppance for the performance we're putting on, and that we might be surprised at the outcome of our charade. What do you think she meant by that?"

"I don't have a clue," Cable said. "Maybe she was implying that we'd get caught. You know, that the matchmakers would figure out what we're doing, just the way she has. That's not a cheerful thought. They'd pounce again with the tuna-fish casseroles. Oh, man, spare me."

Cable drove into the driveway at Lindsey's house and turned off the ignition to the Land Rover.

"Cable," Lindsey said, "my truck is at your house. I need to go over there and drive it back here."

"Oh. Yeah. I forgot."

"We can do that later if you'd like to come in and have a dish of ice cream," Lindsey said, unsnapping her seat belt. "I'd appreciate it if you would, Cable. I need to settle down about Aunt Charity being so ill. If I sit in my house alone, I'll just worry and stew. You'd be doing me a big favor by staying a while."

"It will be my pleasure, ma'am," he said. "What kind of ice cream?"

"Mint chocolate-chip."

"Sold," Cable said, opening the car door. "Lead me to it."

A short time later they were sitting at Lindsey's kitchen table with bowls filled with large servings of the promised dessert. Cable was making short work of his portion, while Lindsey just stirred hers absently, staring off into space.

"You're making soup out of that," Cable said, looking at her bowl.

"I guess I really don't want it." Lindsey sighed. "I was thinking about Aunt Prudence. What will become of her if Aunt Charity—"

"Hey, don't," he said, reaching over to trap one of her hands with one of his on the top of the table. "Aunt Prudence is stronger than you're giving her credit for. Besides, Aunt Charity is a fighter. If anyone can beat that pneumonia, she can."

Lindsey nodded, then sniffled, no longer able to win the battle over the tears that had been threatening ever since she and Cable had been at the hospital.

"Ah, Lindsey." He got to his feet and came around the table to grip her shoulders and urge her up and into the comfort of his embrace. She went willingly, wrapping her arms around his back as he held her close.

And there, encircled in the warmth and strength of Cable's arms, nestled against his solid, powerful body, she cried.

Lindsey wept. Because she was so very worried about dear Aunt Charity.

Lindsey wept. Because she was so confused at

times about her strange and foreign emotions regarding Cable.

Lindsey wept. Because Cable was there, offering her solace, making her feel safe and protected, and allowing her to give way to her tears without passing censure.

Lindsey wept. Because for the first time in a long, long time she wasn't alone and lonely.

And then she stopped. With a wobbly sigh and a little hiccup, she drew a steadying breath and tilted her head back to look up at Cable, who met her gaze.

"Thank you," she whispered. "Just...thank you."

"Feel better?" he said, smiling at her warmly and not releasing his hold on her.

"Much better," she said. "Everything just sort of piled up on me in a big stack and...don't look at me. My face gets all blotchy and weird when I cry, and I know my nose is red and—"

"You're beautiful when you cry," Cable said, starting to lower his head toward hers. "You're beautiful when you *don't* cry." His lips were a fraction of an inch from hers. "Bottom line? You're a very beautiful woman, Lindsey Patterson."

Cable's mouth melted over hers in a searing kiss that she responded to in total abandon. She pressed her hands more firmly onto Cable's back, bringing him closer to her, wanting to feel every rugged inch of him. She parted her lips to allow his tongue to delve into her mouth, savoring the taste of mint chocolate-chip ice cream.

At this moment, she thought hazily, she refused to think about all the things that were upsetting her. She was going to just feel, just be, just cherish. This was natural and right and real. This was Cable. And she wanted him. Tomorrow be damned. All that mattered was this tick of stolen time.

Lindsey broke the kiss and took a sharp, much-needed breath.

"Cable," she said softly, close to his lips. "I want you. I want to make love with you now, tonight. Right now."

"Are you certain of that?" he said, his voice gritty with passion. "You're upset. Maybe you're not thinking clearly and you'll regret taking this step. I couldn't handle that, Lindsey."

"I won't be sorry. I promise. This is natural and right and real...for me. But it has to be for you, too, remember?"

"Oh, yes, I remember. Natural." Cable glided his lips over Lindsey's. "Right." He outlined her lips with the tip of his tongue, causing her to shiver at the sensuous foray. "And very, very real."

He captured her lips in a kiss that was so intense

it caused her to tremble in his arms. Without breaking the kiss he swung her up into his arms and she entwined her hands around his neck. He raised his head slowly, reluctantly, and met her smoky gaze.

"Should we?" he said, smiling. "Or shouldn't we?"

"Oh, Cable," she said, matching his smile. "We should, and we will, and this night is ours. It belongs to us, only the two of us…together."

## Chapter Eight

Cable carried Lindsey in his arms from the kitchen to her bedroom.

This was so romantic, she decided dreamily, as she nestled her head on Cable's shoulder. It was far beyond any daydreaming she might have indulged in in the past, and definitely did not come under the boring heading of woolgathering.

In the bedroom, Cable set Lindsey on her feet and she snapped on the small lamp on the nightstand, casting a soft, rosy hue over the room. She swept back the blankets on the bed to reveal white sheets sprinkled with a pattern of pink rosebuds.

Lindsey watched Cable as he unclipped his holstered gun from his belt and set it on top of the dresser.

"Your badge," she said. "I just realized that it didn't poke me at all."

Cable smiled. "Well, I guess that means that some magic is coming into play here. What do you think?"

"I think," she said, matching his warm smile, "that you're absolutely right. Oh, Cable, this is our little world, just ours, together and, yes, it's very, very magical."

Cable nodded, closed the distance between them and drew Lindsey into his arms. He kissed her so tenderly, so reverently, that tears misted her eyes.

They ended the kiss and stepped back, their hands clasped, then sliding free with a lingering touch of fingertips.

Clothes seemed to float away, a barrier between them not to be endured a moment longer. They stood naked before each other in the rosy glow of the lamp, visually tracing every glorious inch within their view.

"You are," Cable said, his voice gritty, "so very beautiful, Lindsey."

"And you're magnificent, Cable," she said, her voice hushed. "I feel so feminine, so...so cherished."

"You are."

Cable lifted her into his arms again, laid her in the center of the bed, then followed her down, catching his weight on one forearm as he stretched out next to her. He splayed one hand on her flat stomach, then captured her mouth in a searing kiss.

Lindsey wrapped her hands around Cable's neck, inching her fingers into his thick, dark hair, urging his mouth harder onto hers as their tongues met and stroked in her mouth, then his.

The embers of desire within them burst into raging flames that licked throughout them, hotter, burning, causing hearts to race and their breathing to become labored, echoing in the quiet room.

Cable broke the kiss and shifted to one of Lindsey's breasts, drawing the soft flesh into his mouth and laving the nipple with his tongue. Lindsey closed her eyes, savoring the sensuous sensations that were sweeping through her. She pressed her hands onto Cable's broad back, relishing the feel of the taut muscles bunching and moving beneath her palms.

Cable paid homage to her other breast, then moved lower, trailing a ribbon of kisses across her stomach. His muscles quivered from forced restraint and his arousal was heavy against her.

A sigh of pure feminine pleasure escaped from

Lindsey's lips. A groan of masculine need rumbled deep within Cable's chest.

They kissed, caressed, explored and discovered, rejoicing in all that was revealed to them. The flames of desire licked higher and hotter until they could bear no more.

"Oh, Cable, please," Lindsey said finally, her voice a near sob.

"Yes. I want to protect you, Lindsey. I'll be right back."

Hurry, Lindsey's mind hummed. She'd waited an eternity for this night, and every second that Cable was away from her was too long. Hurry, Cable, please.

Cable returned to her, moved over her and entered her, thrusting deep within her. Then he stilled and their smoky gazes met, inches apart.

It was a special moment that spoke of mutual desire and respect, of wishing to give as well as receive. A moment that was theirs alone in their magical world.

Cable began to move, slowly at first, then increasing the tempo in perfect synchronization with Lindsey. Hotter. Higher. The rhythm pounding, causing them to cling to each other as they thundered toward the summit of their exquisite journey.

It was ecstasy. It was far beyond what either had ever experienced before. It was magic.

And then they were there, seconds apart, flung up and over the top into wondrous oblivion.

"Cable!"

"Lindsey. Ah, Lindsey!"

Cable collapsed against her, then mustered his last ounce of strength to move off her before he crushed her, nestling her close to his side. He rested his lips on her dewy forehead, then drew a ragged breath.

"Unbelievable," he said hoarsely. "It was…you were…forget it. I don't have the words to describe…well, hell."

"I know," Lindsey said, sifting the fingers of one hand through the moist, dark curls on Cable's chest. "It was so…I feel…never mind. I don't think the words have been invented yet. That's why we can't find them."

"Mmm," Cable said, smiling.

They lay quietly, allowing their heartbeats to return to normal and heated bodies to cool. Cable reached down and pulled the sheet and blanket over them. Sleep began to creep over their senses, and Cable stiffened, forcing himself to become fully awake.

"What's wrong?" Lindsey said dreamily, opening her eyes.

"I just realized that my vehicle is parked in your

driveway and your truck is still at my house. If I don't get out of here, the matchmakers are going to be a very confused bunch of ladies when they compare notes in the morning.''

"Let them be muddled," Lindsey said. "I don't want to move. I don't want you to go, either, Cable. This is our magical night, remember?"

Cable dropped a quick kiss on her lips. "I'm not about to forget that fact, ma'am. I don't want to leave you, Lindsey."

"Good. Then don't." Lindsey paused. "Oh, dear, what about Buddy?"

"He'll be all right. There's water and food on the patio in the backyard, you've got those plastic-covered things in front of the plants, and it's a warm summer night. How's that? I've just convinced myself that it's fine if I stay right here."

"It's more than fine," Lindsey said, her hand resting on Cable's chest sliding lower…and lower.

Cable took a sharp breath, then chuckled. "You're starting something I'll be only too glad to finish, Ms. Patterson," he said.

"Oh, I hope so, Sheriff Montana," Lindsey said. "I certainly hope so."

Much, much later they slept, heads resting on the same pillow, each tucking the memories of their magical night into special places in their hearts and minds.

\* \* \*

The next morning Lindsey and Cable stood in the kitchen, blowing on the hot coffee in their mugs, trying to cool it enough to drink it as they glanced often at the clock ticking away on the wall.

Lindsey laughed. "This is ridiculous. I refuse to go out that door without having had my coffee, but it's so hot I can't drink it. Oh, good grief, look at the time."

"Well, if a certain woman hadn't crept into a certain man's shower, we wouldn't be in this dilemma," Cable said, smiling, then blew on the coffee again.

"True. I'm guilty. I'm terrible. I should be ashamed of myself." Lindsey laughed. "But I'm not. So there."

"No regrets?" Cable said, suddenly serious.

"No, Cable," she said, smiling at him warmly. "No regrets. I promise."

"Good. That's good." He frowned at the hot drink in the mug. "This isn't working."

"Ice cubes," Lindsey said. "It's the only solution. We'll pop ice cubes in the coffee. That should cool it enough to make it drinkable."

At long last the coffee was consumed and they drove to Cable's so Lindsey could retrieve her truck. Their conversation during the ride centered on Aunt Charity and the hope that she was showing some improvement in the light of the new day.

In Cable's driveway, Lindsey opened the door of her truck, then turned to look up at Cable.

"What do I say at this point?" she said, frowning slightly. "Have a nice day? Thanks for the fantastic night? I'm obviously not up on the proper etiquette involved in the morning after."

"Then let me enlighten you." Cable framed Lindsey's face in his hands and kissed her deeply, causing a flash of heat to swirl low in her body. "There."

"Oh." Lindsey laughed and drew a much-needed breath. "Gracious."

"You can say that again," Cable said, nodding.

"Gracious," she said, smiling.

"Have a nice day, Ms. Patterson," Cable said, then pulled his Stetson low on his forehead. "I'm off to tend to my dog."

"And I'm late for work. Goodbye, Cable."

"I'll call you later," he said.

Cable watched Lindsey drive away, waving as she tooted the horn before disappearing from view.

Incredible, he thought. The lovemaking he'd shared with Lindsey had been...well, incredible. She was a passionate woman, held nothing back, gave of herself completely. Their lovemaking had been...yes, natural and real and very, very right.

It had been a long time, if ever, since he'd felt so emotionally connected to a woman. It had been so important to him that he give Lindsey pleasure during their lovemaking, that he meet her needs.

Magic, he mused, as he turned and started slowly toward the backyard. That was what he and Lindsey had declared their night together to be, the world they'd created for themselves. And it had been.

And now? In the ever-famous morning after? He wanted to make love with Lindsey Patterson again. And again. And again. But he also wanted to see Lindsey's smile, hear her wonderful laughter, stay by her side as they weathered the storm of worry about Aunt Charity's illness.

He liked being with Lindsey, enjoyed her company, respected and trusted her as a woman, a person.

Trust, Cable thought, as he approached the gate to the yard. Damn. He still believed that Lindsey was hiding something from him, possessed a secret she was not willing to share. It centered, somehow, on her adamant stand never to marry, he was sure of it.

Would she ever tell him that deep, dark secret? Would she come to trust him that much? He hoped so, he truly did. It was important to him for reasons he still couldn't quite fathom.

Cable's wandering thoughts were cut short as he entered the backyard, his eyes widening. Buddy came bounding across the grass, yipping and wagging his tail. Cable swept his astonished gaze over the yard.

Every one of the two-foot-high, scallop-topped wire enclosures was lying flat on the ground in front of the bushes. Not one had been left standing.

"You," Cable said, narrowing his eyes and looking down at a bouncing Buddy, "are the dog from hell."

Buddy barked, then began to chase his tail in a dizzying circle.

A short time later, Cable entered the office building with Buddy straining on the leash in front of him. Mary-Margaret pursed her lips and stuck her nose in the air when the pair stopped by her desk.

"Uh-oh," Cable said. "You're in your mad mode, Mary-Margaret. What am I guilty of?"

"As if you don't know," Mary-Margaret said with an indignant little sniff.

Cable leaned toward her. "Give me a hint."

"What I'll give you is a piece of my mind," Mary-Margaret said. "You and Lindsey must have laughed yourself silly when you cooked up your plan.

"The telephones were ringing all across town bright and early this morning with the tantalizing news flash that Sheriff Montana's vehicle had been at Lindsey Patterson's house all night.''

''Oh,'' Cable said, nodding.

''Then,'' Mary-Margaret rushed on, ''the bulletin was also spread that Lindsey's truck had been at *your* place all night. Do you realize how many minds you've boggled? That was *not* nice, Cable Montana.''

''Well,'' Cable started.

''Not nice at all,'' Mary-Margaret said, glowering at him. ''I figure you were both in your own houses, sleeping like babies in your own beds, and just switched the vehicles to confuse those who have your best interests at heart. This is serious business, Cable.'' She smacked the desk with one hand and Cable cringed. ''This…is…not…a… game. Am I making myself clear?''

''Yes, ma'am, you certainly are,'' Cable said. ''You bet.'' He paused. ''So, um, you believe that Lindsey and I were in our own homes and alone in our own beds, huh?''

''I wasn't born yesterday. You're not dealing with a dum-dum here, Cable.''

''You're right,'' he said, stroking his chin with one hand. ''You're not a dum-dum, Mary-Margaret. In fact, I think that the conclusions you came to regarding me, Lindsey and the night in question are quite interesting, even borderline amazing.''

"Yes, well, just don't pull a stunt like that one again," Mary-Margaret said. "Now then, go see Pete at the pizza parlor. Someone tried to jimmy the lock on the back door of the place last night, but didn't get in. What do you suppose they wanted to steal? Pepperoni?"

"Naw," Cable said. "They were after the dough." He frowned as Mary-Margaret stared at him with a rather blank expression on her face. "That was a joke, Mary-Margaret, sort of a pun thing. Get it?"

"Goodbye, Cable."

"Right."

"Yes or no?" Glenna-Sue said to Lindsey.

Lindsey blinked. "Pardon me?"

"I swear, Lindsey," Glenna-Sue said, shaking her head, "you may be here in body, but you left your mind somewhere else when you came to work this morning."

"Oh, well, I…" Lindsey started.

Glenna narrowed her eyes. "Are you so preoccupied because you're cooking up another scheme like the vehicle switcheroo you pulled with Sheriff Montana last night? That was so mean of you two.

I hope you know you confused a great many people with your shenanigans.''

"We did?'' Lindsey said, producing an expression of pure innocence. ''Gosh, Glenna-Sue, I'm terribly sorry if we upset anyone.''

"You are not,'' she said. ''You think you're very clever, but we figured it out once we gathered all the facts. I certainly hope you won't do such a silly thing again. I mean, my stars, Lindsey, all we want is for you and Cable to be happy.''

"But you feel that we won't be happy unless we're together,'' Lindsey said. ''A couple. A twosome. A...whatever. Right?''

"A *married* couple,'' Glenna-Sue said decisively. ''A *married* twosome. A husband and wife. That's the ticket to your and Cable's happiness. One needs only to see you two together to know that.

"You shouldn't be wasting time by playing nonsensical games like you did with those vehicles last night. We all know now that you were each in your own home...alone. You can't cuddle with your shadow, Lindsey Patterson.''

"You can't cuddle with your shadow,'' Lindsey said thoughtfully. ''That's very profound and very true, isn't it? Is it a famous quote?''

Glenna-Sue shrugged. ''I just made it up. Not bad, huh? Anyway, you get my point.'' She paused. "Is there any fresh news about Aunt Charity?"

"She's a little bit better," Lindsey said, "but not out of the woods. Her temperature is down another degree, but Ben is still very concerned. We all are."

"Including me," Glenna-Sue said. "I do hope Aunt Charity will be all right. The mere thought that she might—no, I can't even dwell on it for a second or I'll cry. I'm changing the subject. Did the wire barriers you put in front of Cable's bushes do the trick as far as keeping Buddy out of trouble?"

"I forgot to check," Lindsey said, "but Buddy would have to be a wonder-dog to have dug those things up. I'm sure the problem has been solved."

"Well, that's good. Oops," Glenna-Sue said, as the telephone on the front desk in the nursery rang. "I'm coming, I'm coming."

Lindsey wandered down one of the rows of plants in the large rear area of the nursery, snipping off leaves that didn't meet her approval.

You can't cuddle with your shadow, her mind echoed again. No, you couldn't. When you were alone, you were alone, pure and simple. Which was fine. Which was how she would spend the remainder of her days…and nights. Which was something she'd come to grips with long ago.

And which was suddenly the most depressing thought she'd ever had in her entire life.

"Lindsey Patterson," she said aloud, "just cut it out, knock it off, quit."

Facts were facts and nothing would change them. Not daydreaming, not woolgathering, not exquisite lovemaking with the most magnificent man she had ever met. Her relationship with Cable was temporary and would end, be over, done, finished, in a few weeks.

After that she'd pack up the memories of what she'd shared with Cable, tuck them into a corner of her heart, and get on with her life…alone.

And in the meantime? She was going to savor every moment with Cable, feel feminine and special, cherished and beautiful, and so very, very alive.

She'd told Cable that she had no regrets about the momentous, intimate step they'd taken together, and that was the truth. She wasn't sorry about last night. Oh, no, far from it.

Granted, there had been a multitude of emotions tumbling through her along with the heated desire, but those emotions, just like the time remaining with Cable, were temporary, would fade into oblivion when Cable exited stage left from her life.

So, yes, okay, she *had* entertained the fleeting thought that being with Cable might be dangerous, that she was running the risk of possibly falling in love with him and ending up with a shattered heart.

"Nope," Lindsey said to a small pine tree in a bucket. "Won't happen. I'm in control, doing great."

*You can't cuddle with your shadow.*

Lindsey pressed one fingertip to her forehead.

"Go away," she said. "I'm erasing that statement from my memory bank. It's history. Poof. It's gone."

"News, news, I have news," Glenna-Sue said, bustling down the aisle toward Lindsey.

"What? What?" Lindsey said, turning to smile at her. "It must be good, because you're beaming, Glenna-Sue."

"Oh, it is," Glenna-Sue said, puffing for breath as she stopped in front of Lindsey. "Jennifer MacKane, who is now Jennifer MacKane Mac-Allister, her husband, Jack, and their two boys, Joey and Jason, are flying in from California because of Aunt Charity being so ill."

"Oh, that's marvelous," Lindsey said, smiling. "That ought to perk Aunt Charity up. It will be wonderful to see all of them, and none of us have met Jason yet."

"That baby is about ten months old already," Glenna-Sue said, "and Joey must be…heavens, he's got to be six years old. Time is just rushing

by.'' She paused and frowned. ''Lindsey, you
don't think that Aunt Charity will believe she's not
going to get better, do you? I mean, what with
family flying in from the coast and all?''

''No, I don't think Aunt Charity would jump to
that conclusion.'' Lindsey laughed. ''She'll simply
enjoy being the center of attention. She'll want to
get her hands on that baby she hasn't held yet, and
you know she's crazy about Joey. This visit will
be just what the doctor ordered, as the saying
goes.''

''And won't our lovely visitors be surprised and
pleased to hear that you and Sheriff Montana are
a couple?'' Glenna-Sue said, clasping her hands
beneath her chin. ''Oh, my, they'll be so thrilled.''

''Go answer the telephone, Glenna-Sue,'' Lindsey said, frowning.

''It's not ringing.''

''It will eventually,'' Lindsey said. ''I'm going
to water some plants.''

''You watered when you first arrived this morning, Lindsey,'' Glenna-Sue said. ''Remember?
Like I said before, you are so preoccupied today.
Of course, a man like Cable Montana is certainly
capable of consuming one's total thoughts, isn't
he?''

''The telephone, Glenna-Sue,'' Lindsey said,
pointing toward the front of the nursery.

"Yes, dear. However, I would suggest that you check with me before you do anything back here so I can tell you if you've already done it."

"I'm not going to survive this," Lindsey said, rolling her eyes heavenward as Glenna-Sue hurried away. "Yes, I will. Anything is better than tuna-fish casseroles with peas."

## Chapter Nine

Lindsey stood in the middle of Cable's backyard, her hands on her hips as she swept her gaze over the disaster that Buddy had created.

"I don't believe this," she said. "I know, I know, I'm seeing it with my own eyes, but I really don't believe that one furry little dog could...I don't believe this."

Cable took off his Stetson, raked one hand through his hair, then yanked his hat back onto his head, pulling it low on his forehead.

Buddy was running in a circle around the pair, barking at full volume.

"What can I say?" Cable said. "The situation is hopeless. No matter what I do, Buddy is one step ahead of me. I think he was an entire demolition derby in a former life."

Lindsey laughed. "Now there's a thought." She paused, perplexed. "The question is what brilliant idea do we try next?"

"I don't have a clue," Cable said. "We're supposed to be on our way to dinner right now, then we're going to the hospital to visit Aunt Charity. But what am I supposed to do with the beast? If I leave him here in the yard, there won't be a single bush left standing by the time we get back."

"Well," Lindsey said, tapping one fingertip against her chin, "what if we leave him in *my* backyard? There's nothing there for him to damage. It's all decorative gravel and I haven't taken the time to put any plants in yet. We can put his food and water on the patio and take along some of his toys, too. How's that?"

"Sounds like a plan," Cable said, nodding. "Which is more than I have."

"How do you feel about mixing cement?" Lindsey said. "That's the only way you're going to be assured he can't dig up those wire barriers if we set them back into place."

"Hell," Cable said. "Well, so be it. I'll hire ol'

Ralph McDuff to do it. He's always looking for odd jobs to earn a little extra money.''

"Cable," Lindsey said, looking up at him, "did it ever occur to you that Buddy gets into so much trouble because he's bored? He spends all this time with you, then, boom, he's alone and his companion—you—is gone. A bored boy is mischief waiting to happen.''

"What do you want me to do?" he said, frowning. "Get him a subscription to *Sports Illustrated,* or buy him his own television set?''

Lindsey laughed. "Don't get crabby. I just wonder if he might be happier if he had a playmate. You know, another puppy to hang out with. Maybe there's one left from the litter.''

"You're kidding," Cable said. "No, you're not kidding. You're really serious? You're suggesting I have *two* of these monsters driving me nuts?''

Lindsey shrugged. "It was just a thought. Everything you've come up with so far hasn't done the trick. I mean, good grief, Buddy ate a playpen, among other things. Maybe he just isn't meant to be alone.''

Cable looked at Lindsey intently, a rather perplexed expression on his face.

"What?" she said, flipping out her hands palms up and hunching her shoulders.

"What you said just sounds strange coming

from you, I guess,'' Cable said, frowning. ''You sure are quick to join the rank and file of the matchmakers with this notion that he's lonely and needs a partner in life. That's your solution for him? *You're* suggesting this? Ms. Independent I-don't-need-anyone Patterson?''

''For heaven's sake, Cable,'' Lindsey said, matching his frown, ''I'm talking about a puppy having a playmate. It has nothing to do with me, personally. You're comparing apples and oranges here.''

''No, I'm not,'' he said, his volume rising. ''That's where your mind went with no hesitation. Buddy is lonely. Why doesn't that outlook pertain to you? Why are you so dead set against marriage, commitment, having a partner to share with in *your* life?''

''I've told you that I—''

''No,'' he said, slicing one hand through the air. ''Don't dish out your pat answer of being too busy with your business, not having time to devote to a relationship, being too independent, and all that malarkey. That spiel doesn't work for me, Lindsey, not even close.

''You know and I know that there's something else going on with you that you're not telling me. Come on, Lindsey, after all we've shared together, don't you think it's time that you trusted me enough to tell me the truth?''

Lindsey took a step backward and wrapped her hands around her elbows. She averted her gaze from Cable's and stared down at the toes of her shoes.

No, she thought frantically. She couldn't bare her soul to Cable, she just couldn't. The thought of seeing pity in his eyes, then the withdrawal, the anger, the physical and emotional distance he would put between them, was more than she could bear. She couldn't relive that nightmare again. Not again.

Oh, why was he doing this? They had created a magical world that was so perfect, was theirs for such a short tick of time. Why couldn't Cable just leave it alone, let them savor what they had while it was theirs?

Lindsey drew a steadying breath, then looked at Cable again, lifting her chin in a defiant gesture.

"My, my, Sheriff Montana," she said, "it would seem that your male ego is suffering a bit of a blow. I'm not falling all over you, trying to snare you into the marriage trap or whatever, so you figure I have to have a secret agenda, or some such thing.

"I mean, gracious, I couldn't possibly be a healthy single woman who just isn't interested in a long-term relationship with you, could I? You're accustomed to females who take one look at you and start sighing wistfully as they turn the pages in bride magazines.

"Well, guess what, Montana?" Lindsey rushed on, none too quietly. "You and I are engaged in a short-term affair and that's all I'm interested in, thank you very much. Put that in your testosterone pipe and smoke it."

Cable nodded slowly as he crossed his arms over his chest.

"Okay, have it your way...for now," he said, a muscle jumping in his jaw. "But I'm going on record as saying that I don't believe your well-practiced story."

Cable laughed, the sharp sound holding no humor. "Want to hear some good old-fashioned truth from *me?*" he said, a rough edge to his voice. "The fact that you don't trust me enough to tell me what's really going on with you hurts. It does, Lindsey, just like a punch in the gut. I don't know why it should matter so much to me, but it does, it really does. There. That ought to stroke your *feminine* ego to the max."

"This isn't a contest of egos, Cable," Lindsey said quietly, meeting his gaze again. "This isn't a game with a score card. Yes, we're playing out a charade when we're in public, but—" she shook her head "—what we're sharing together when we're alone is real. It's ours. Don't ruin what we have in our magical world, Cable. Please don't do that."

"I don't want to, believe me," he said, sounding weary. "But how else should I feel when trust is missing from that magical world?"

"I don't know what more I can say to you to convince you that I..." Lindsey stopped speaking and stared into space.

She mustn't say any more, she told herself frantically. To do so was to bring an enormous lie into the magical world that belonged to her and Cable. To continue to deny that she had a secret she refused to share with Cable was going to tarnish the perfection of what they had together.

Lies were powerful, had strength beyond measure, could crumble all they had into dust, leaving no precious, beautiful memories for her to keep. And she wanted those memories, needed to have them to cherish in the months and years ahead when she would once again be alone.

No, she couldn't cuddle with her shadow, but she could wrap herself in warm memories of what she had had with Cable Montana when the nights were too long and cold, dark and lonely.

"Cable," she said, shifting her gaze to just above his left shoulder, "are you ready to take

Buddy to my house, then go to dinner? We don't want to be too late getting to the hospital and miss out on visiting Aunt Charity.''

Cable took a deep breath, then let it out slowly, puffing his cheeks.

''Okay, I don't have to get hit with a brick,'' he said. ''The subject is closed, for now.''

''No, Cable, the subject is closed, period. There's nothing further to discuss.''

''We'll see,'' he said, then whistled. ''Buddy, come on, you felon. Let's pack up your food and toys. You're going to a place that is indestructible, even for you.''

During the drive to Lindsey's house she held Buddy, allowing him to stand on her lap and poke his head out the window to enjoy the wind rushing by. She slid a glance at Cable, saw the tight set to his jaw and stifled a sad sigh that threatened to escape from her lips.

Everything was getting so very complicated, Lindsey thought dismally. The last thing on earth she'd ever wanted to do was hurt Cable Montana, yet that was exactly what he'd said she was doing by refusing to share her innermost secret with him.

That he cared for her, about her, enough to be suffering pain from her silence was startling, to say the least. And fantastic, and wonderful and—

No, no, it was foolish to dwell on that amazing fact, because in the long run it didn't mean a thing. Once the charade was over, their goal accomplished, she'd be out of sight, out of Cable's mind. He'd soon forget her and any deep secret he was convinced she had.

Buddy barked, pulling Lindsey from her troubled thoughts.

"You tell 'em, kiddo," she said to the puppy. "Let the bad guys know that the sheriff's lean, mean dog is on duty, by golly."

Cable chuckled. "Yeah, right. Buddy would be a big help during an arrest. He'd probably lick the perp into submission."

"You're not sorry you got Buddy, are you?" Lindsey said, looking over at Cable. "I realize that he has caused you a great deal of trouble since you got him, but you love him, don't you?"

"Sure, I do," Cable said, nodding. "I don't regret adopting Buddy. I've wanted a dog since I was a kid. My mother is allergic to any kind of furry pets, and after I was out on my own I always lived in apartments until now. I've waited a long time to have Buddy. We'll work out the kinks and be the dynamic duo, a man and his dog."

"Hear that, Buddy?" Lindsey said. "If you shape up, you might be an official deputy sheriff of Prescott, Arizona."

"There you go," Cable said, then paused. "You know, Lindsey, something you've yearned for, wanted for a very long time is worth fighting to keep, doing everything within your power to make it work."

"I agree," she said, frowning slightly, "but am I missing a message here? Are you referring to something other than your puppy?"

"No," Cable said quickly.

Or was he? he thought in the next instant. Where in the hell had that profound statement come from anyway? He'd just opened his mouth and said it without thinking and he had a sneaking suspicion it didn't pertain to Buddy at all.

Man, he was losing it. Big time.

He'd had no intention of telling Lindsey that her failure to trust him enough with her secret was causing him emotional pain. But there he'd stood in his backyard, spilling out his feelings to her like an idiot.

And now? Had what he'd just said about not giving up on something important when the going got tough come from that same place deep within him?

Ah, hell, what was this woman doing to him?

He did *not* want to become involved in a long-term, serious relationship with anyone. And he sure as hell never intended to marry again. No way.

What he had with Lindsey Patterson was temporary, a means to an end, and would be over very soon. That was the way it was and the way he wanted it.

Wasn't it?

"Damn it," Cable said, not realizing he'd spoken aloud.

"Damn it...what?" Lindsey said.

"Huh? Oh. I, um, just remembered something I forgot to do before I left the office," he said. Now *he* was lying through his teeth, for cripes' sake. "It's not important. Would you like to have Italian food for dinner?"

"Sure," Lindsey said, nodding. "Would you?"

"That's fine. Italian food is fine. I like Italian food. You bet. It's great stuff that Italian food."

"Cable, you're babbling," Lindsey said. "What on earth is the matter with you?"

Cable drove into Lindsey's driveway and turned off the ignition to the Land Rover.

"Nothing is wrong with me," he said dryly, "that a brain transplant wouldn't cure."

"Oh, okay," Lindsey said, laughing as she opened the car door. "Buddy, you poor baby, your daddy just announced that he's a cuckoo."

Buddy barked, then began to jump straight up in the air when Lindsey set him on the ground.

"Takes one to know one, I guess," Cable said,

watching the dog's performance. "Buddy and I are a matched set."

Buddy was a lucky puppy, Lindsey mused, as they gathered up the dog's supplies. Cable was determined that he and the dog would be just fine together, that they'd work through the problems that Buddy was currently creating. Cable had made a commitment to that furry bundle and had no intention of breaking it.

Long after she was out of Cable's life, was nothing more than a fading memory, if even that, the man and the dog would still be together. Oh, yes, Buddy Montana was a very blessed little guy.

Lindsey sighed, a rather wistful, sad-sounding sigh that caused Cable to look at her questioningly as they headed for the backyard.

"When you order your brain transplant?" Lindsey said. "Make it two. I think I'm becoming a candidate for one myself."

"Ah, so what are you saying, ma'am?" Cable said, grinning. "That you and I are a matched set, too? Now there's a news flash that would send the local matchmakers straight into seventh heaven. We're a matched set. Remember that phrase, Lindsey. Maybe we'll get a chance to whip it on one of the dear old ladies. It's great dialogue for the charade."

"Our charade needs all the help it can get," she

said, as they entered the backyard. "The masses were furious over what they decided was a naughty trick we pulled with our vehicles being at each other's houses all night. They believe we were each in our own bed, alone, snoozing away."

"I know," Cable said, chuckling. "I caught hell about that all over town. Well, when we're at the restaurant tonight, gaze deeply into my eyes and sigh. Can you produce a rather dreamy, sappy expression on your face?"

"Me? Why do *I* have to do it?" Lindsey said, placing Buddy's bowls on the patio.

"I'll do my share," Cable said, dropping the puppy's toys next to the bowls. "I'll...yeah, I'll poke a bread stick in your mouth so you can take a bite. That's corny enough to appear romantic."

"Oh, please," Lindsey said, rolling her eyes heavenward. "Spare me. Let's go for a long, lingering look as we touch our wineglasses together in a toast. The matchmakers will have oodles of fun deciding what the toast actually was. Not bad, huh?"

Cable nodded. "Not bad at all." He looked down at Buddy. "Okay, sport. Enjoy. I'm not even going to tell you to stay out of trouble, because there's no trouble you can get into in this yard."

The Italian restaurant had been decorated in a classic motif with red-checked tablecloths and dripping candles in wicker-covered, chunky wine bottles. The lights were kept dim, allowing the candlelight to cast a soft glow over the rather small expanse.

It was a popular place to eat and Lindsey and Cable were seated at the last available table, having nodded and smiled at people they knew as they were led to the table set against the far wall. The waitress handed them menus and said she'd return in a few minutes.

"Great location," Cable said, glancing around the crowded room. "Everyone saw us come all the way across here." He looked at Lindsey. "You're positive you won't go for a dreamy, sappy expression? We've got a very attentive audience, you know."

"Forget it, Montana," Lindsey said, laughing as she held the menu in front of her face. "I'm deciding what I want for dinner."

"Okay, try this," Cable said. "We'll compromise. Lose the sappy and just go for dreamy."

"Lasagna," Lindsey said, peering at him over the top of the menu.

"What?" Cable said, frowning in confusion.

"I'm ignoring your compromise proposal," Lindsey said. "I'm going to order lasagna."

Cable chuckled. "All right. I know when I'm

beat. Lasagna sounds good to me, too. There we go again...being a matched set.''

"Give it a rest,'' Lindsey said, laughing.

The waitress appeared at their table and beamed.

"My, my, aren't we a happy couple this evening?'' she said. "It's so nice to see you two together and to witness your pure unadulterated joy.'' She sighed wistfully. "It just warms my heart, it truly does.''

"That's nice,'' Cable said, unable to curb his laughter. "May we place our order now?''

While they waited for their food, Lindsey asked Cable if he knew that Jennifer and Jack were coming over from California to see Aunt Charity, although she wasn't certain when they planned to arrive.

"No, I hadn't heard that news,'' he said, "but it's great. Aunt Charity will be very pleased, I'm sure. Do you know Jack and Jennifer?''

"I only met them once,'' Lindsey said, "just before they left for California. Jennifer hired The Green Thumb to keep up the yard at her house while it was for sale. It sold so quickly that I didn't have that much to do. They seemed like very nice people and that Joey is a sweetheart. Of course, they have another son now, too.''

"Yep. Jason,'' Cable said. "That MacAllister

clan just keeps on getting bigger and bigger. There's a whole bunch of those folks."

"They must have such fun at family gatherings," Lindsey said. "It would be noisy and nuts, and there would be kids running all over the place, and everyone would be having a wonderful time and..." She stopped speaking and smoothed her napkin in her lap. "Anyway, it's very nice of Jennifer and Jack to make a special trip to visit Aunt Charity because she's ill."

"You'd like to be part of a large family like the MacAllisters, wouldn't you." Cable said, more in the form of a statement, than a question.

Lindsey met Cable's gaze again with a rather nondescript expression on her face.

"Oh, I think it sounds good on paper, as the saying goes," she said, shrugging, "but in actuality those get-togethers are probably bedlam and everyone goes home thoroughly exhausted, hoping there isn't another one scheduled too soon on the calendar."

Before Cable could reply, the waitress appeared with their dinner.

Nice try, Lindsey, he thought, as the food was placed on the table, but no cigar. Damn it, he'd heard the longing in her voice when she'd spoken of all the MacAllisters being together. But now she was scrambling to the opposite extreme, making it clear that a large, noisy, loving family held no appeal for her.

Lindsey and her secret, Cable mused. It was causing the knot of pain in his gut to hurt with a greater intensity because she refused to share it with him.

"There you are," the waitress said, bringing Cable from his thoughts. "All set?"

"It looks wonderful," Lindsey said, smiling. "Thank you."

"Enjoy your dinner," the waitress said, "and holler if you need anything. I won't disturb you unless you signal me. I know you want to be left alone. Together. The two of you. With no interruptions."

"You bet," Cable said, nodding. "We appreciate your thoughtfulness. Don't we, Lindsey?"

"Oh, my, yes," Lindsey said quickly. "We certainly do. Appreciate. Your thoughtfulness. Yes."

The waitress smiled, then hurried away.

Cable laughed and shook his head.

"As far as your being an actress goes," he said, "don't quit your day job."

"I never said that I'd be good at this," Lindsey said, smiling, "but it really doesn't matter because people will see and hear what they want to believe anyway. My crummy performance will pass with flying colors."

"True," Cable said, filling their glasses with red wine from the carafe. "Let's do our romantic toast bit, then we'll call it quits for now, just relax and enjoy, be ourselves."

"Perfect," Lindsey said, lifting her glass to touch it against Cable's.

"To…magic," he said quietly, looking directly into Lindsey's eyes. "*Our* magic."

"Magic," Lindsey whispered.

With their eyes never leaving the other's gaze, they took a sip of the sweet wine, then set the glasses on the tablecloth.

The candlelight flickered, casting golden hues over their faces. The sounds of conversation and laughter in the distance disappeared, along with the clink of silverware on dishes.

They were alone in their magical world, far, far away from the small Italian restaurant. Desire began to churn and burn within them, fanning embers still lingering into leaping flames that consumed them. But there was a gentleness, too, in this magical place that caused soft smiles to form on their lips.

There was, Lindsey thought hazily, a dreamy, sappy expression on her face, she just knew it. But she didn't care, because no one was here to see it but Cable. Oh, he looked so ruggedly handsome in the candlelight, so male, so magnificent, so…hers.

They were together on this night and that was all she cared about. Magic.

Lindsey, Cable's mind hummed. She was so beautiful with the candlelight pouring over her. Her cheeks were flushed with the hue of a soft peach and her lips were beckoning to him to kiss them. He was on fire. The coil of heat low in his body was increasing, tightening with every beat of his racing heart. Now, right now, this woman was his. And it was magic.

"Cable," Lindsey said, her voice sounding strange to her own ears, "our dinner is getting cold."

"Our what?" he said, shaking his head slightly. "Oh!" He cleared his throat and very slowly, very reluctantly, shifted his gaze to his plate. "Well, we'd better...we'd better dig in, don't you think?"

Lindsey nodded and picked up her fork, ignoring the fact that her hand was trembling.

Dear heaven, she thought, she was a breath away from bursting into tears. She felt so strange, so shaken, so emotionally out of control.

What on earth was the matter with her? She didn't know, but whatever it was, enough was enough. She was getting a grip, remembering that she and Cable were out in public, that they were playing out their roles in the charade.

"I'm doing fine," she said, not realizing for a

second that she'd spoken aloud. "What I mean is, this lasagna is fine, delicious."

"Really?" Cable said. "How can you say that when you haven't taken a bite yet?"

"Oh." Lindsey popped a forkful of the lasagna into her mouth, chewed, swallowed, then nodded. "Yummy."

They ate in silence for several minutes, each lost in their own thoughts.

"You know, Lindsey," Cable said finally, "there *is* something, well, magical between us at times. It's hard to describe, to define, but it's there. I've never experienced anything like it before."

"No, I haven't either," she said softly, "but there's no point in attempting to discover what it is, because what we're sharing is temporary, Cable."

Cable nodded. "Yeah, you're right, I guess. This charade will be over soon. We'll stage our big breakup and the matchmakers will leave us alone to nurse our broken hearts. No more tuna-fish casseroles—with or without peas. Then we'll each go about our business like we were before all this nonsense started. That will be great, huh?"

"Super," Lindsey said dismally. "I'll devote myself to The Green Thumb, and you and Buddy will go around catching all the bad guys. Yep, things will be back to normal and life will be just dandy.''

"Mmm," Cable said, then pushed his plate away. "I'm not as hungry as I thought I was."

Lindsey put down her fork. "I can't take another bite. My stomach was bigger than my eyes, or however that saying goes. I think I said it backward."

"Well," Cable said gruffly, "the folks watching us in here will go nuts with this one. We're so much in love we've lost our appetites. That ought to cause a buzz." He paused. "Lindsey, why did we suddenly lose our appetites?"

Lindsey glanced quickly around, then leaned toward Cable.

"I have no idea," she said, "but it certainly isn't because we're so much in love as you so profoundly put it. It will appear that way to our eager audience, but it isn't remotely close to the real reason why I couldn't choke down another bite if my life depended on it. Maybe we're catching the flu."

"The flu," Cable said, frowning. "No, I never get the flu."

"Well, whoopee for you," Lindsey said, matching his frown. "It wouldn't diminish your machismo if you did, you know. It's a very human thing to do."

"So is falling in love," Cable said, his voice

very low, and very rumbly and very, very male. "What if that is what is happening here, Lindsey, to us?"

Lindsey sank back in her chair and folded her arms across her breasts.

"Don't be ridiculous," she said, glaring at him. "To even suggest such a thing means you're getting caught up in the charade, losing touch with what's real and what isn't. Get a grip, Montana."

"I'm perfectly aware of where the charade starts and where it ends, Ms. Patterson," he said, narrowing his eyes. "Where the waters get muddy is when we're alone, when that strange magic takes over and—"

"Cable, don't," Lindsey interrupted. "We agreed that it was foolish to explore that, remember? There's no point in it. We'll simply enjoy what we have together while it's ours to have, then it will be over and...I think it would be best if we ended this conversation." She pushed back her chair and got to her feet. "Let's go to the hospital and visit Aunt Charity."

Cable stared up at Lindsey for a long moment, then got to his feet. He placed several bills on the table, then looked at Lindsey again.

"All right, we'll go over to the hospital and see how Aunt Charity is doing," he said. "But there's something you need to be aware of."

"Oh?"

"I'm a cop. I don't like unsolved mysteries. I like concrete data and definite answers. I just might decide to figure out…the magic."

"Go for it," she said, waving one hand breezily in the air. "But I'm going on record as saying I don't wish to discuss this again. Understand?"

"You're coming across loud and clear, ma'am," Cable said, grinning. "Smile at me. Our public is watching this exit."

"Oh, for Pete's sake," she said, rolling her eyes heavenward. "This whole thing is so bizarre."

Lindsey closed the distance between them, flung her arms around Cable's neck and planted a loud, smacking kiss on his lips, causing his eyes to widen in shock.

"Oh, take me home, honey-bun," she said loudly. "I simply can't wait even another second to have you all to myself."

"You betcha, baby-cakes," Cable said, encircling her shoulders with one arm. "We're outta here."

They looked at each other and burst into laughter. Then to the accompaniment of wistful sighs and a smattering of applause they left the restaurant with Lindsey nestled close to Cable's side.

## Chapter Ten

The trip to the hospital was short but very, very sweet. Lindsey and Cable met Ben Rizzoli in the lobby and he informed them that Aunt Charity's temperature was just above normal, she'd been taken off the oxygen and was sleeping peacefully.

Jennifer and Jack, Ben also said, had arrived from California and visited Aunt Charity. The patient was now nagging Ben unmercifully to be allowed to go home so she could see Joey and that baby, Jason, whom she hadn't had a chance to even hold yet.

They returned to Lindsey's home and, standing in the driveway, Cable put a finger to his lips.

"Shh," he said. "Listen."

"I don't hear anything," Lindsey whispered.

"That's my point. There hasn't been a peep out of Buddy since we got here. That means he's sleeping."

"Sleeping the sleep of the innocent?" Lindsey said, smiling.

"That's pushing it a bit," Cable said, chuckling, "but I guess he qualifies tonight at least. We know he couldn't get into any trouble in your backyard."

"Nope, my yard looks like a parking lot," Lindsey said. "Let's go inside and take a peek at Buddy out the kitchen window just to be certain that he's all right."

"Spoken like a true mother," Cable said, sliding one arm across Lindsey's shoulders. "You have those natural, maternal instincts."

"No, I don't."

Lindsey started quickly across the yard toward the front door, causing Cable to drop his arm to his side and stride forward to catch up with her.

"Hold it," he said, stepping in front of her. "What just happened here? I said something about you being a natural-born mother and I felt you tense up so fast it's a wonder you didn't break something. Would you care to explain?"

"Oh, it's just a pet peeve of mine," Lindsey said, peering into her purse for the key to the house. "People, especially men, have a tendency to think that just because a woman is...well, a woman, that she automatically is bonkers about babies and can step right up and take care of a slew of them. There are, however, some women who just don't have any desire to be a mother."

"And you're one of those?" Cable said, following her into the house. "Part of the group who doesn't want to have children?"

Lindsey snapped on a lamp, shrugged, then turned to face Cable, not meeting his gaze directly.

"I haven't given it that much thought," she said. "Are you hungry yet? I have cookies, ice cream, popcorn, all kinds of goodies."

Cable placed his Stetson on the back of the sofa. "No. No, thank you, I'm still not the least bit hungry. How about you?"

"No," Lindsey said, wrapping her hands around her elbows. "No, I'm not hungry." She paused. "Would you like to watch a movie on television? Play gin rummy?" She lifted her chin. "Or would you like to make love to me for hours? I want to make love with you, Cable, because I don't want to think anymore tonight, I really don't. I just want to feel, just be. What do *you* want to do?"

Cable stared at Lindsey for a long moment as he digested what she had just said. A smile began to form on his lips, a lazy, all-male smile that caused a delicious shiver of anticipation to slither down Lindsey's spine.

"Well, now, ma'am," Cable said, running his hand over his chin, "you've given me some interesting choices here, I must say. Gin rummy is fun. But then again, I should save up any luck I might have with cards for when I play with Aunt Charity, because she wipes me out."

Lindsey nodded thoughtfully, then proceeded to unbutton the light blue cotton blouse she wore over navy slacks. "Aunt Charity will be looking for a gin rummy game once she gets home."

Cable swallowed heavily as Lindsey's blouse hit the floor, followed by her bra. She slowly, so slowly, began to undo the back zipper of her slacks.

"Don't let me distract you from making your choice from the list of available activities, Sheriff," she said, wiggling so the slacks would slide down her legs. She stepped free of them and her shoes. "Take all the time you need."

Heated desire exploded within Cable with such intensity it momentarily stole his very breath, causing his voice to be raspy when he spoke.

"You, Ms. Patterson," he said, "are a pro at avoiding topics you don't wish to discuss. You're also wonderful, and crazy, and unpredictable, and fantastic and…and you have three seconds to—'' he opened his arms to her ''—come here.''

Lindsey laughed in pure delighted joy and flung herself at Cable. He caught her in his arms and lifted her off her feet as he captured her lips with his. The kiss was fire, licking flames of passion that consumed them instantly, causing their hearts to race.

Cable slid Lindsey slowly and sensuously down his body without breaking the kiss. When her feet touched the floor, he lifted his head slightly to take a ragged breath.

''I do believe, sir,'' Lindsey said, her voice trembling with desire, ''that you have too many clothes on.''

''This is how I usually dress,'' Cable said, then trailed a ribbon of nibbling kisses along Lindsey's throat, ''to play gin rummy.''

''Ah,'' she said. ''So you've made your choice of how you intend to spend the evening? Shall I go get the playing cards?''

''On second thought,'' Cable said, releasing his hold on her, ''I really do think I should wait to play gin rummy with Aunt Charity.'' He pulled his knit shirt over his head and dropped it onto the floor, then unclipped the pager from his belt and set it on the back of the sofa. ''Don't you think that's a good idea?''

Lindsey slid her hands up Cable's chest, entwining her fingers in the moist, dark curls and savoring the feel of the taut muscles beneath.

"Mmm," she said. "It would be very thoughtful of you to wait to play cards with Aunt Charity."

"I'm a thoughtful guy."

"You're a slow-as-molasses guy," Lindsey said with a wobbly little laugh. "Cable, if you don't hurry up, I think my bones are going to dissolve. I want you so much. I don't care if that's pushy, or brazen…or… It's honest and real and there's no other way for me to say it."

"I want you, too, Lindsey Patterson," he said, swinging her up into his arms. "We are most definitely a matched set."

In Lindsey's bedroom, she snapped on the lamp, swept back the blankets on the bed and skimmed off her panties as Cable shed his remaining clothes. They tumbled onto the bed, an urgency engulfing them, a hunger and need that caused a whimper to escape from Lindsey's lips and a groan to rumble in Cable's throat.

There was no rational thought, only exquisite, sensuous sensations and the heat, the incredible heat that burned hotter with every beat of their racing hearts.

Hands were never still and lips followed where hands had been, creating heated paths along a body soft and a body muscled and hard. It was a strange, unexplainable mixture of discovering the new along with the wondrous sense of familiarity, of being where they belonged.

It was magic.

And they knew it, and they rejoiced in the knowledge.

Time lost meaning as they savored the taste, the feel, the aroma of each other, their senses heightened like never before. They reached the edge of their control, yet still held back, waiting, anticipating what was to come, until they could bear no more.

"Cable, please," Lindsey whispered.

He left her only long enough to take steps to protect her, then returned to capture her lips in a searing kiss, his tongue delving deep into the sweet darkness of her mouth. She met his tongue boldly with her own, dueling, dancing, stroking.

He moved over her and into her and she sighed in pleasure as she splayed her hands low on his back to urge him closer, to fill her, to bring to her all that he was.

The tempo of their union was thundering, nearly rough in its intensity, pounding, pleasing both, carrying them deep into the spiraling heat that churned around them and in them, lifting them up and away, carrying them closer and closer to where they wanted, *needed*, to go.

They were flung over the top in an explosion nearly shattering in its intensity. They called each other's name, clinging, holding fast, so as not to be swept into oblivion without the other.

It was ecstasy beyond their wildest imaginations.

And it was magic with the brilliance of a million stars created just for them.

They hovered, floated, memories etching themselves indelibly into hearts and minds. The bed was there to catch them as they drifted down. The room returned to their views. Reality edged the sensual mist gently and slowly aside, allowing them the luxury of tender caresses and nipping kisses before the last of their strength was gone.

With sated sighs of contentment and awe, they lay close, not speaking, simply cherishing what they had just shared.

And then they slept.

"Damn it!"

Lindsey shot bolt upward on the bed, her heart racing as she was jolted awake by Cable's angry bellow. She glanced quickly at the empty expanse of tangled sheets next to her on the bed, looked at the clock to see that it was just after six in the morning, then cringed when Cable repeated his roaring expletive.

"Cable?" she called. "Where are you? What are you swearing about?"

Cable appeared in the bedroom a few moments later. He was fully dressed and his hair was damp, indicating that he'd already showered. His jaw was dark with an overnight beard, and his eyes were narrowed in fury.

"What?" Lindsey said, drawing the sheet up to cover her bare breasts.

"You don't want to know," he said gruffly, dragging one hand through his hair and leaving tracks where his fingers burrowed.

"Oh, okay," Lindsey said, nodding. "I'll just assume that you woke up in this chipper mood for reasons I'm never to know."

Cable sighed. "It's Buddy. Lindsey, he dug a hole in your backyard. He made a mountain of gravel, went through the plastic tarp beneath, and went halfway to China. He's covered in dirt and he's so pleased with himself he's wiggling like a windup toy."

Lindsey's eyes widened in disbelief, then in the next instant she burst into laughter. She sank back onto the pillow and laughed so hard she had to wipe tears of merriment from her cheeks.

Cable walked slowly to the edge of the bed,

folded his arms across his chest and watched her fall apart, a frown on his face.

"Oh, my," Lindsey said finally, gasping for breath. "I just sort of lost it there. But your description of what Buddy did was priceless and the look on your face was..." She waved one hand in the air. "No, don't get me started again. Oh, what a funny bit."

"You won't think so when you see the mess in your backyard," Cable said dryly.

Lindsey sat up again, tucking the sheet under her arms. "Oh, Cable, Buddy is just a baby. He'll outgrow this naughtiness." A bubble of laughter escaped from her lips. "I think. I hope."

"Darn it, Lindsey," Cable said, chuckling and shaking his head. "I was rather enjoying being on a mad-as-hell rip, but it's impossible for me to do anything but smile when I hear the sound of your laughter. It could bring sunshine to the cloudiest day."

"What a lovely thing to say," Lindsey said, smiling up at him. "Does that mean you've forgiven Buddy?"

"I suppose. I'll go fill in the hole in your yard, then take the monster with me. I've got to get home, shave, put on my spiffy uniform and hit the road to the office."

"What about breakfast?" Lindsey said.

"I'll grab something on the way to work." Cable paused. "Last night was...I don't have the words to describe how I feel, Lindsey."

"I don't either, Cable," she said softly. "It was...well, I guess we both know that it was very beautiful and special."

Cable leaned down and dropped a quick kiss on the top of her head. "Bye for now."

"That's it?" she said, laughing. "That's all I get? A peck on the head?"

"Yep," he said, starting toward the bedroom door. "If I do anything more, I'll end up late for work. Guaranteed. I have no willpower whatsoever when it comes to you, Ms. Patterson. See ya."

"See ya," Lindsey whispered, then sank back onto the pillow with a contented sigh.

She allowed the memories of her lovemaking to float into her mind in sensuous, vivid detail.

"Gracious," she said, as she felt the flush on her cheeks. "Go to work, Lindsey."

She tossed back the blankets and left the bed, making no attempt to curb her smile as she headed for the shower.

Just before lunch, Lindsey had received a telephone call at The Green Thumb from Megan Rizzoli, inviting her and Cable to a cookout at their house that night.

Now, the group, including Andrea, Brandon and their baby, as well as Jennifer and Jack MacAllister and their kids, ate on the back patio of the Rizzoli house. Joey appointed himself in charge of a leashed Buddy, which included, to his mother's dismay, sharing his dinner with the exuberant puppy.

Ben announced that he was releasing Aunt Charity from the hospital the next day with strict instructions that she was to do nothing more than rest in her and Prudence's apartment at Hamilton House. "I told her that if she didn't follow my orders," Ben said, "I wouldn't allow Joey, Jason and Ashley to visit her. That ought to do it."

"You're a tough guy," Megan said, smiling. "Mean and lean."

"No," Ben said, laughing. "I just know how stubborn and independent Aunt Charity can be. I had to play all my aces at once to get the upper hand. It's going to take a while for Aunt Charity to get her strength back, and she must get the rest she needs. I'm counting on Aunt Prudence to scold Charity if she cheats."

"I'm just so grateful that Aunt Charity is going to be all right," Jennifer said. "When we got the call that she was so ill, I felt as though we were a million miles away. All I could think about was getting here as quickly as we could." She paused.

"Jack, can you hear Joey? He said he was going to take Buddy for a walk around the front of the house, but I don't hear them coming back and it's starting to get dark."

Jack got to his feet and plunked Jason onto Lindsey's lap. "I'll go get him," he said. "I hope you realize that we won't be able to postpone getting Joey a dog after this visit. Either that or we could kidnap Buddy and take him home with us."

Cable laughed. "You really don't want to do that, Jack. Buddy is a disaster waiting to happen. Be kind to yourself and leave the beast with me."

"Oh, okay," Jack said, laughing as he started toward the front of the house.

Lindsey stared at the baby who had suddenly appeared on her lap. "Hi," she said to Jason. "You sure are cute. You're also sitting on the lap of someone who knows zip about babies, but I imagine you'll let me know if I don't hold you the way you want me to." She leaned closer. "You smell so good, like a sweet, sweet baby boy."

"You look very natural with Jason on your lap, Lindsey," Cable said quietly. "You two make a very nice picture."

Before Lindsey was forced to think of something to reply to Cable's heart-tugging statement, Jack came running into the backyard.

"Look at this," he said, holding up Buddy's

leash. "The collar is still buckled and attached to the leash. I think Buddy slipped out of the collar, took off and Joey went after him."

Everyone got to their feet, Lindsey holding Jason close to her.

"Oh, God," Jennifer said, the color draining from her face. "It's almost dark, Jack, and there are dense woods surrounding this area. We've got to find Joey. Now. Right now."

"Did you see any tracks?" Cable said.

"No," Jack said. "Nothing."

"Okay, let's stay calm," Cable said. "I'll get on the radio in my vehicle and tell my deputies to report here. Maybe Joey and Buddy will show up five minutes from now and the deputies won't be needed, but I'd rather do too much than too little. We'll get organized and start a search."

"I'll get a flashlight," Ben said. "Megan, you and the women take the babies inside. Brandon, Jack, I've got extra flashlights you can use. The more manpower we have, the better."

"Cable?" Jennifer said, her voice trembling.

"We'll find Joey," Cable said, gripping her shoulders. "He'll be back here safe and sound before you know it. My men are trained in search and rescue. We'll map out the territory and every inch will be covered. Just hang tough for me, okay?"

Jennifer nodded as she struggled against threatening tears. Jack hugged her tightly for a long moment, then headed off with Ben and Brandon to get the flashlights.

"Let's go into the house," Megan said. "We'll wait in there. Everything is going to be just fine, Jennifer. Joey will be back in your arms complete with wiggling puppy before it's even time for Joey to be put to bed."

But neither Joey nor Buddy were safely returned that quickly. Two hours later, Cable radioed Mary-Margaret and told her to put out the word that volunteers were needed from town to search for a missing Joey in the woods surrounding Ben Rizzoli's house.

A short time later the vehicles started to arrive with men equipped with flashlights and women with thermoses of coffee. The road leading to Ben and Megan's house was lined with official police vehicles, pickup trucks, cars and even a motorcycle. The people of Prescott had turned out in force to find the missing boy and the puppy who was with him.

Jason and Ashley fell asleep and were put on Ben and Megan's bed, surrounded by fluffy pillows.

Cable coordinated the search, giving one man in

each team a walkie-talkie. Mick, as the head deputy, was to stay behind at the house and receive the calls from the various groups, keeping in contact with everyone who was out searching.

The house was crowded with women, who began to make sandwiches from fixings Megan provided so the men could rest and eat in shifts if needed.

"I'm heading back out with a fresh group of men," Cable said to Lindsey. "Take it easy. You're pale as a ghost."

"This is so terrifying, Cable," she said. "It's so dark out there and it's getting chilly and…you'll find them soon. Right? You will, won't you, Cable?"

Cable gathered her into his arms. "We'll find them. I promise you that, and I never make a promise I know I can't keep."

"I'll be waiting right here for you, Cable," Lindsey said. "Be careful. Please, please be careful. There's very treacherous terrain out there and…" She shook her head as tears choked off her words.

"I'll watch my step," he said. "This nightmare will be over very soon, you'll see. We'll be back with a tired little boy and an exhausted puppy. And you'll be waiting for me. That's good, Lindsey. Yeah, that's…that's really good."

Cable released his hold on Lindsey and left the house. She stood staring at the door that Cable had closed behind him, wrapping her hands around her elbows as a chill of fear swept through her.

"Come safely home to me, Cable," she whispered. "Bring Joey and Buddy with you and come home to me. Oh, Cable, please."

## Chapter Eleven

Just before midnight Cable refused to be relieved by the rested men who arrived to replace the four-man group that he was leading.

"No, I'm staying out here until we find Joey, Jasper," Cable said.

"You've got to be mighty tired, Cable," Jasper said.

"I'm fine. Okay, you guys who have been out here head back to Ben's house and get some food and rest. You new fellas wait here a minute while I search the other side of this mountain of boulders."

"Got it," Jasper said. "Watch your step up there. Now that I think about it, I don't see how a little boy could scale rocks that size."

"He probably couldn't," Cable said, "but he might have come in from the other end where it's more level. I need to know that we've covered every inch of these woods."

"Okay," Jasper said, nodding. "We'll direct our flashlights on you to give you as much light as possible. How are you going to climb while you're holding a flashlight in one hand?"

Cable frowned. "Very carefully."

As Cable made his way up the boulders, he slipped several times, finding it difficult to gain purchase on the slick rocks and definitely being hindered by clutching the flashlight.

At last at the top, he flattened on his stomach and shone the light down at the sloping terrain on the other side, seeing only low bushes and a multitude of rocks.

"Joey!" he called. "It's Cable Montana. I've come to take you home. Joey, are you down there, kiddo? Joey? Joey!"

"See anything?" Jasper yelled.

"No, I..." Cable started, then stopped speaking, every muscle in his body tensing. "Joey?"

"I'm here. I'm Joey," a little voice said in the

distance. "I want my mommy. I'm scared and I want my mommy and Buddy is scared, too."

Cable rested his forehead on the rough rock for a moment and closed his eyes.

"Thank God," he whispered. "We found them." He raised his head again and yelled into the darkness. "Joey, keep talking so I can find you with my flashlight. Are you hurt? Where are you?"

"We're not hurt," Joey called, "but we're stuck. We can't get out from between these rocks and…I have to go to the bathroom, and I want my mommy, and it's dark and scary, and I think there's a big, big bug in here." He burst into tears. "I want to go home."

Cable squinted as he moved the flashlight slowly across the area where Joey's voice seemed to be coming from. His heart skipped a beat when the light fell on the little boy who was holding Buddy. The pair was wedged between two large rocks.

"I see you, Joey," Cable hollered, then turned his head to yell at Jasper. "I've got them. Radio to the house and let them know we've found them and they're not hurt. Tell Mick to call the other groups of searchers back to Ben's. I'm going down there to where they're wedged between some rocks. One of you guys come up here with that rope."

''Praise the Lord,'' Jasper said. ''We got ourselves a baby boy and a puppy.''

A loud cheer went up from the men standing by Jasper, then one of them began to climb the boulders with a coiled rope slung over one shoulder as Jasper spoke into the walkie-talkie. Cable began to make his way over the top and down the other side toward a crying Joey and a now wiggling and yipping Buddy.

''Hey, everyone, they found them!'' Mick yelled above the buzz of conversation in Ben and Megan's living room. ''Cable's group has them in their sights and both Joey and Buddy are fine. Cable is going down some rocks to get them right now.''

''Oh, thank God, thank God,'' Jennifer said, then covered her face with her hands and gave way to tears of relief and gratitude.

Megan hurried to lead Jennifer to a chair, as Lindsey pressed trembling fingertips to her lips to stifle a sob that threatened to escape from her throat.

''Cable found them,'' she whispered, nodding jerkily. ''Cable found them, just like he promised.''

As the assembled group began to applaud and

yell their approval of Mick's news, he waved his hand for silence.

"Sorry, Jasper," Mick said into the walkie-talkie, "I didn't get that last transmission. Folks are going nuts here. What did you say? Over."

"Hold on," Jasper said, his voice sounding rather tinny over the walkie-talkie. Several moments passed with crackling static the only noise in the now silent room. "Okay! All right. There he is. Hey, Joey boy, you got yourself a dirty face, little fella. Wait until your mama sees you. She's going to dunk you right into the bathtub. Mick, Joey isn't about to let go of that squirmin' dog. No way. No how. Over."

"We've got a big welcoming party waiting here for both of them, Jasper," Mick said. "Just bring 'em on home. Over."

"Roger that," Jasper said. "Is Miss Jennifer there? I got somebody here who wants to say hello to her."

Jennifer ran across the room and Mick handed her the walkie-talkie, showing her where the buttons were that she'd need to push on the device.

"Mommy?"

"Oh, Joey, yes," Jennifer said, tears streaming down her face, "this is Mommy. Are you all right, sweetheart?"

"I'm kinda cold and I need to go to the bathroom really, really bad, but Cable found me and Buddy and got us, and now we're here and I get to hold this walker-talker thing just like on TV, but I want to see you, Mommy.'' Joey started to cry. "I need a feel-better hug, Mommy, I really do."

"I'll hug you for a zillion years," Jennifer said, sniffling. "I love you so much, Joey."

"I love you, too, Mommy. What? Oh, I'm supposed to say goodbye and over. Goodbye. Over."

"Jasper," Mick said, as Jennifer handed him back the walkie-talkie. "What's your ETA? Over."

"We're about twenty minutes out, I'd guess. We'll hustle this tired pair back to you, believe me. I'll send a couple of guys with Joey and Buddy, while the rest of us haul Cable back up from down the other side of these rocks. Over."

"Roger," Mick said. "I'll contact the other groups and have them come on in. Over and out."

The buzz in the room started again and Lindsey smiled as she swept her gaze over the crowd. There wasn't a dry eye in the place, men included.

No one was making any move toward the door, everyone determined not to leave until they saw Joey and Buddy with their own eyes. She placed one hand on her heart and drew a deep, steadying breath.

Megan came to where Lindsey was standing.

"Oh, what a night," Megan said, smiling, "but we have a happy ending."

"Yes, we do," Lindsey said, matching her smile. "I can only imagine how Jennifer must be feeling. She was so brave and—"

"Quiet please, folks," Mick said. "Say again, Jasper. Over."

"Ah, hell's fire, Mick," Jasper said through the static on the walkie-talkie. "The rope snagged and...damn it all, Cable's taken a bad fall, Mick. The sheriff is hurt, and we need a stretcher out here. He's not moving, Mick. He's just lying down there not moving. We need more rope and more men and...hurry it up, Mick. Over."

"No," Lindsey said, shaking her head. "Don't say that, Jasper. Don't say that Cable is hurt."

Megan gripped one of Lindsey's hands. "Take it easy, Lindsey. Jasper has no way of knowing how seriously injured Cable is. Let's just stay calm until we have more details and—"

"I've got to go outside," Lindsey said frantically. "I want to wait for Cable and...oh, God, Megan, I can't bear the thought of... Cable has to be all right. He just has to be." Tears filled her eyes. "Do you understand?"

"Yes," Megan said quietly, as the people in the room talked among themselves with worried expressions on their faces. "I understand completely,

Lindsey. You're in love with Cable and it's tearing you up inside to think that he's injured out there somewhere. Your reaction is perfectly normal, but please try to calm down a little.''

''I never said that I was in love with...'' Lindsey stopped speaking, sniffled, then took a shuddering breath as she wrapped her hands around her elbows. ''Oh, dear heaven, yes, I *am* in love with Cable. Have I known that but refused to acknowledge my feelings because...'' She shook her head. ''It doesn't matter how I feel, because it's all so hopeless anyway. The only thing that is important now is that Cable is not badly hurt, that he'll be all right.''

Megan frowned. ''What do you mean it's all so hopeless? Anyone who sees Cable with you can tell that he cares very deeply for you. He may even be in love with you for all we know. That certainly doesn't sound hopeless to me. It falls more into the category of romantic and wonderful.''

''No, no, you don't understand. I...'' Lindsey dashed tears from her cheeks. ''I'm going outside, Megan. That will make me feel closer to Cable somehow.''

''But...'' Megan started, then frowned in confusion as Lindsey dashed out the front door. ''You're right, Lindsey Patterson,'' she said to no one. ''I don't understand one iota.''

\* \* \*

During the next hour, Lindsey paced back and forth in the front yard of Megan and Ben's house. It came to light, as men returned from the search, that Jasper had come partway back from where Cable was hurt to lead the paramedics, who had arrived on the scene and set out with a stretcher to the accident site. In the process the group of men with Cable had been left without a walkie-talkie. There was no news of Cable's condition.

She was in love with Cable Montana, her mind repeated over and over. Oh, how had that happened? When had she lost control of her heart, her mind, her very soul?

Forget it, forget it, forget it. There was no point in attempting to determine when Cable had stolen her heart, because nothing was going to come of it anyway. They had no future together no matter how Cable might feel about *her*.

She could not have all that came with love—a husband, home, babies. None of those things were hers to have. Not ever.

Lindsey continued to pace as unnoticed tears streamed down her pale cheeks.

Cable groaned as he was settled onto the stretcher, then jostled as the four men carrying it started away from the boulders.

"You've got yourself a dandy of a headache, I imagine," said one of the men. "You were out cold for a bit there and have a concussion. Not a real bad one, but enough to make you feel like you've been to the party of the century."

"Mmm," Cable said, closing his eyes.

"Your right ankle is pretty bummed up, too," the man went on. "I don't think it's broken, just badly sprained, but they'll check it out for sure at the hospital. You just relax and let us get you back to civilization, Cable."

"Mmm," Cable repeated.

"We ended up without a walkie-talkie," the man said. "We can't let the folks back at the house know you're all right. I bet they're worrying up a storm, especially Lindsey Patterson. Sorry we gummed it up and don't have any way to communicate with your lady."

"Shut up and let the man rest," one of the other men said. "You talk enough for three people at one time."

"Oh, okay," the man said, chuckling. "I won't say another word."

"Mmm," Cable said.

*Your lady,* his mind echoed. Damn, that sounded good. Lindsey Patterson was his lady. Yeah, she was. Right at the moment when he felt himself falling, when he'd had nothing to hold on to but his own emotions, he'd known without a single doubt that he was deeply and irrevocably in love with Lindsey.

Then he'd whopped his head on a rock and went out like a light, but when he came to, there it was...still there...the truth. He was in love with Lindsey Patterson. Because of his Lindsey he'd escaped from the pain of the past and was thinking only of the present and future.

And it was natural, right and real.

And fantastic.

And sensational.

And couldn't these guys move any faster so he could see Lindsey, tell her how he felt, ask her if she loved him and if she did, would she do him the honor of becoming his wife? Oh, man, what a picture that painted in his mind. Beautiful. A life, a future, a forever...with Lindsey.

"Hey, there you are," Ben said, coming toward the group. "I thought I'd meet you and see how the patient is."

"Don't stop walking," Cable said. "I've got something important to do back at the house."

"*Someone* is more like it," Ben said, falling into step beside the stretcher. "Lindsey is a tad upset at the moment." He held up the walkie-talkie he was carrying in his hand. "This one I grabbed is a dud. Wouldn't you know it? We still can't let the folks at the house know you're going to live to see another day, Cable.'' He looked at one of the men. ''What's the word?''

''Slight concussion, sprained, maybe broken ankle,'' the man said, ''and he weighs a ton. Why aren't these hero types ever puny little guys?''

Ben chuckled. ''There you go. Hey, Cable, Joey and Buddy were just arriving at the house when I left to meet up with you folks. I thought Jennifer was going to squeeze the stuffing out of that kid. That is one happy mom.

''Jack came rushing in with his group and Joey, Jennifer and Jack were holding on to each other so tightly it was something to see. Nice work out there, Cable, except for getting yourself bummed up.''

''Yeah, well, I'll survive,'' Cable said, ''if these guys don't rattle the teeth out of my head.'' He paused. ''Lindsey's upset?''

''Big time,'' Ben said. ''She's pacing back and forth in front of the house, staring into the woods, waiting for a glimpse of you. She's crying, too. Megan went outside to try to get Lindsey to come back into the house, but I don't think Lindsey even heard her talking. There are times when a person cannot reason with a woman who is in love.''

''Amen to that,'' one of the men said. ''They can get really weird.''

"A woman who is in love?" Cable said, a grin breaking across his face. He frowned an instant later. "Oh, damn, my head."

"How's your heart?" Ben said, smiling. "Floating around where Lindsey's has gone to?"

"No doubt about it," Cable said. "We're a matched set from the sound of things. How much longer before we reach the house?"

"I can see the lights up ahead," Ben said. "Ten minutes maximum, I'd say."

Ten minutes, Cable thought. Then he'd see her. The woman he loved. The woman who, hopefully, loved him. The woman he wanted to spend the remainder of his days with. His lady. His Lindsey.

The majority of the people who had been in the house had moved outside to await the arrival of Sheriff Montana. Lindsey stood apart from the crowd and no one approached her, everyone seeming to sense that she wished to be alone.

A sudden cheer went up from the group and Lindsey jerked at the loud noise. In the distance she saw the bobbing beams of flashlights. Standing on tiptoe she caught a glimpse of the men carrying the stretcher on which she knew Cable lay.

A murmur rippled through the crowd then a man shouted above the voices. "Cable is all right," the man hollered, cupping his hands around his mouth.

''Slight concussion, maybe a busted ankle, but he's going to be fine.''

Applause and yells of approval filled the night air. Women hugged each other and men slapped their buddies on the back.

Lindsey dashed tears from her cheeks with trembling hands and willed her racing heart to quiet its tempo.

''Thank God,'' she whispered. ''Cable is alive and he's going to be all right and—''

''Lindsey?'' Glenna-Sue said, coming to where Lindsey stood alone. ''Honey, are you okay? Don't you want to move around all these people and go greet Cable?''

''No,'' Lindsey said, a sob catching in her throat. ''No, Glenna-Sue, I just needed to know that Cable was all right. Could you take me home. Please? Please, Glenna-Sue? Could you drive me to my house now? Right now?''

Glenna-Sue frowned. ''That doesn't make any sense, Lindsey. You want to leave before you even speak to Cable? Why would you do that?''

''Please, I can't explain it,'' Lindsey said, shaking her head. ''I just need to go home. I'll ask someone else to take me if you don't want to, but I've got to leave here, Glenna-Sue, I do.''

''Well, all right then, if that's what you want,'' she said, still frowning in confusion. ''Come on.

I'll drive you into town and see you safely into your house but…are you positive this is what you want to do?''

"Yes, I have to," Lindsey said, sniffling. "I really do. Please tell Megan we're leaving. Hurry, Glenna-Sue, just hurry."

Cable lifted his throbbing head and scanned the crowd, looking for Lindsey. He was oblivious to the press of people surrounding the stretcher, offering praise for finding Joey and expressing the hope that Cable would be fit as a fiddle in no time.

When the pain forced him to lower his head again, he sighed in frustration that he hadn't yet seen Lindsey as the men began to level him into the ambulance. He saw Megan speak close to Ben's ear, then Ben climbed into the ambulance after Cable was settled.

"Let's roll," Ben told the driver.

"Wait just a damn minute," Cable said. "Where's Lindsey, Ben? Get her in here so she can ride to the hospital with me. I need to see her, talk to her."

"Take it easy, Cable," Ben said quietly, as he sat down on a bench against the inside of the ambulance. He looked at the driver. "Go."

The driver turned on the ignition to the ambulance and started away from the house and the crowd of people.

"Damn it, Ben," Cable roared. "Oh, hell, my head. Forget my head. Where is Lindsey?"

"Cable," Ben said. "Megan told me that Lindsey waited until she saw your stretcher come into view, then asked Glenna-Sue to take her home."

"What?" Cable said, pressing the heels of his hands to his temples.

"Look," Ben said, "I can't say I truly understand why Lindsey left when she did, but you have to remember that women are very complex creatures.

"Maybe she didn't want you to see her crying, or maybe she knew she'd really come unglued when she saw you and she didn't want to do that in front of so many people, or—hell, I don't know, but I'm sure that Lindsey will explain it to you when she sees you. Okay?"

"No! It's not okay," Cable said, then closed his eyes for a moment as pain rocketed through his head and ankle. "Something is very wrong here, Ben. I've got a cold knot in my gut that says that something is very, very wrong."

## Chapter Twelve

Cable Montana was not a happy man.

When he opened his eyes in the hospital the next morning, he was exhausted due to the fact that he'd been wakened every hour during the night by a nurse, who had asked him mundane questions to be certain there were no lingering effects from his concussion.

He'd finally bellowed that he would arrest the next person who asked him who the president was, causing the nurses to flip coins to see who lost and had the dangerous duty of waking the grumpy sheriff.

He needed a shower and a shave, Cable mentally fumed, some clean clothes and a hefty serving of food that was fit to eat.

And he needed to see Lindsey Patterson.

Cable shifted on the uncomfortable bed. He cringed as his left ankle, which was bound in an elastic bandage after X rays had determined that it wasn't broken, objected to the movement by shooting a jolt of pain up his leg. His head throbbed like a toothache.

He elevated the bed, bringing him to a sitting position, then pressed hard on the call button to a nurse.

He wanted out of there, Cable thought fiercely. Right now. Ben Rizzoli had insisted that he be admitted to the hospital for the night and, by damn, Dr. Rizzoli had better be prepared to set him free.

If not? Hell, he'd walk out of this place whether his discharge papers were signed or not, that's what he'd do. And that bullheaded stunt would probably get him tossed in the slammer by one of his own deputies, because even the sheriff couldn't get away with walking around town buck naked, and he didn't have a clue as to where his clothes were.

"Hell," Cable said, frowning and pressing harder on the call button.

The door to his room opened and Ben entered,

pushing a fully dressed Aunt Charity in a wheel-chair.

"Lay off the call button, Montana," Ben said, stopping Aunt Charity's wheelchair at the side of the bed. "You're not the most popular patient in this place as it is. The nurses are drawing straws to see who gets the unwanted duty of giving you a sponge bath."

"Over my dead body, Rizzoli," Cable said, glowering at Ben.

"Well, okay, if that's what it takes," Ben said, shrugging.

"I am not having a bath in a damn bowl," Cable yelled, then pressed both hands to the sides of his head with a groan.

"Hello, big boy," Aunt Charity said cheerfully. "You're not feeling too sunny this morning as far as I can see. Me? I'm on top of the world. You may be stuck in this joint, but I'm going home."

"So…am…I," Cable said, narrowing his eyes and staring at Ben. "Isn't that right, Rizzoli?"

"Yeah," Ben said, laughing. "I was only kidding about the sponge bath. I'll go sign your discharge papers right now, which will earn me points with the nurses on duty. Andrea and Brandon are coming to pick up Aunt Charity. They can give you a lift home, Cable."

"Where's my vehicle?" Cable said, then

paused. "How's Joey? Who had the dubious honor of keeping Buddy overnight?"

"Your deputies took your vehicle to your house," Ben said, "but you can't drive it. You can't put that kind of pressure on that ankle.

"Joey is no worse for wear and is having a grand time relating the tale of his big adventure, having survived a stern lecture from Jennifer about taking off after Buddy in the first place.

"Buddy spent the night at the Rizzoli hotel. He was as good as gold. You sure have done a fine job of training that little guy, Cable."

"Are we talking about the same dog? Mine? Buddy Montana?" Cable said, raising his eyebrows. "Unbelievable. Forget that. Let's go back to a vehicle for me to drive. I need to borrow a car from someone who has automatic transmission."

"Come on, Cable," Ben said. "You have to take it easy for a few days. You've got a concussion, remember, and a badly sprained ankle. You can lounge around your house and get all caught up on the talk shows and soaps."

"Not a chance," Cable said.

"From what I hear," Aunt Charity said, "you need to have a serious discussion with Lindsey, and the sooner the better."

"Damn straight," Cable said. "Does Megan

need her car today, Ben? Or maybe Andrea will loan me hers.''

"You're hopeless," Ben said. "You're still going to pay my bill even if you don't follow my orders. I'll go sign you out of here.''

Ben left the room and Cable leaned his head back on the pillow and closed his eyes.

"Listen, hotshot," Aunt Charity said, "you'd better work on your mood before you see Lindsey or you'll blow it. I was right, wasn't I? That performance you and Lindsey were putting on for the matchmakers caught up with you. You two fell in love with each other while you were playing your silly game.''

Cable sighed and lifted his head. "I've got a cold knot in my gut that says you might be only half right, Aunt Charity. Oh, yeah, I'm in love with Lindsey. I won't deny that. I don't *want* to deny it. But Lindsey? After the way she took off last night I just don't know if she...'' He stopped speaking and shook his head.

"You gotta talk to her, dum-dum," Aunt Charity said. "I heard how she hightailed it home last night without speaking to you, but you don't know why she did that. The word is that Lindsey was very upset about you being hurt, it was late, she was tired. Go see what she has to say for herself this morning. She didn't go to The Green Thumb, by the way.''

"She didn't?'' Cable said, frowning.

"Nope. She called Glenna-Sue and told her to get the part-timers in and cover the nursery. Lindsey is holed up at home. Borrow a car and get your cute tush over there.'' Aunt Charity paused. "*After* you shower and shave, of course. You look like a bum.''

"Aunt Charity,'' Cable said quietly, "you are a very wise woman. Why do you think Lindsey left last night before seeing me?''

Before Aunt Charity could answer Cable's question, Ben came back into the room.

"Okay, here's the scoop,'' Ben said. "Aunt Charity, Brandon and Andrea are here to take you to Hamilton House, where you will do exactly what I've told you, which means you will do nothing but rest.''

"That's a thrill a minute,'' Aunt Charity said.

"Cable,'' Ben said, "Megan is on the way over to loan you her car. She said she'll enjoy having an entire day at home to play with Buddy. I'll drive her back to our house when she gets here.''

"Good,'' Cable said. "Thank you, Ben. I really appreciate it.''

"You can wear your grungy clothes from last night to leave here,'' Ben went on. "They're hanging in the closet over there. Stay off that bummed-up ankle as much as possible, let me know if you suffer any dizziness or blurred vision from your bump on the bean, and never get hurt again, because I don't think the nurses will allow you back in this hospital.''

"Mmm," Cable said.

"Off we go, Aunt Charity," Ben said, gripping the handles of the wheelchair. "Say goodbye to the grump in the bed."

"Remember, big boy," Aunt Charity said, as she and Ben headed for the door, "don't mess it up. Take a deep breath, calm down, and, for Pete's sake, smile when you see Lindsey. Got that?"

"Yes, ma'am," Cable said sullenly. "I'll smile like a toothpaste commercial, but I *will* get the answers to my questions."

"Chill out," Aunt Charity called over her shoulder, as Ben pushed her wheelchair through the doorway. "Your entire future happiness may be at stake here, Montana."

"That's what I'm afraid of," Cable said to the empty room. "Ah, Lindsey, what the hell is going on? What's wrong, my lady? What's wrong?"

Lindsey cringed as she stared at her reflection in the bathroom mirror.

She was paying a price for her night of wailing

her head off, she thought dismally, but she just hadn't been able to stop the flow of tears. Now her eyes were puffy and her clogged sinuses were killing her.

She sighed and wandered toward the kitchen, wondering absently if her upset stomach would tolerate another cup of coffee.

The really crummy part, she thought, as she sank onto a chair at the table with a mug of coffee, was that the hours of weeping hadn't solved a thing, hadn't produced a magical solution to her hopeless situation.

No, the facts were still etched in stone and always would be. She'd fallen in love with Cable Montana, lost her heart to the most magnificent man she had ever known, and absolutely nothing could come of it. It made no difference how Cable might feel about her, because even if he was actually in love with *her* they had no chance of a future together.

"I know that," Lindsey said aloud, then sniffled. "Ohhh, I'm so miserable, so sad, so...ohhh."

The doorbell rang, causing Lindsey to nearly spill the coffee at the sudden noise. Her eyes widened as she got slowly to her feet.

Cable? she thought frantically. Dear heaven, what if that was Cable at her door? She wasn't ready to face him yet, not yet. She was too emotionally devastated, would never get through a confrontation with Cable without falling apart.

She moved quickly to the front window in the living room and peered through the shutters. She couldn't quite see her porch from where she was, but recognized Megan Rizzoli's car in the driveway. The doorbell was pressed again, very insistently.

Okay, she thought. Maybe it would help to pour out her heart to Megan, tell her the truth, then swear her to secrecy. Perhaps talking to another woman would be comforting.

Lindsey opened the door, saw Cable standing before her, gasped and slammed the door closed again. An instant later Cable pounded on the door.

"Lindsey!" he yelled. "Open the damn door! I want to talk to you. Right now. Lindsey!"

"Go away," Lindsey whispered, flapping her hands at the closed door. "Oh, please, Cable, just go away."

"I'm not moving from this spot," Cable roared. "I'm a wounded man, Lindsey Patterson. I'm in excruciating pain, but I'm not budging."

Lindsey flung the door open. "You're in pain? Oh, my gosh, that's terrible. Come in, come in."

"I should hope so," Cable said, glaring at her as he limped into the house.

"Sit down," Lindsey said, her eyes widening as

she saw that Cable's left foot was clad in only a sock. "Is your ankle broken?"

Cable sank onto the sofa. "No, it's only sprained, a fact you would know if you hadn't disappeared last night." He sighed. "Ah, hell, Lindsey, what's going on? What's wrong? Why didn't you want to see me last night?"

Get a grip, Lindsey told herself. She had to reach deep within herself and produce the performance of a lifetime. She had to.

She drew a steadying breath, then walked around the sofa and settled onto an easy chair.

"It wasn't that I didn't want to see you last night, Cable," she said, looking at a spot about three inches above his head. "I mean, gracious, I was very worried when I heard you were injured. But once I knew you were all right, I realized that the best thing to do was leave."

Cable narrowed his eyes. "Why?"

"Why?" Lindsey cleared her throat and kept her gaze averted from Cable's. "We both know from playing out the charade what a terrible actress I am. All those people would have been watching me greet you when they carried you in on the stretcher. I never could have pulled off a touching reunion scene." She shrugged. "So, I left and came home."

The cold knot in Cable's stomach tightened to the point of sharp pain.

"I see," he said quietly.

"This isn't all bad, now that I really think about it," Lindsey rushed on. "I suppose the matchmakers are wondering why I left before speaking to you, too. This can be our big breakup number that we planned, and that will be the end of the story."

"Is that what you want, Lindsey?" Cable said, his voice raspy.

She examined the fingernails on one of her hands. "The timing is good to end our charade. The scene is set, know what I mean? It was all very fun, Cable, and I enjoyed our outings and…and everything we…we shared, but enough is enough, don't you think?"

"I'm not sure what I think," he said, staring at her intently. "Answer me this, Lindsey. Why have you been crying?"

"Crying?" she said, looking directly at him. "Me? Who said I've been crying?"

"One look at your eyes tells me what I need to know." Cable leaned toward her and rested his elbows on his knees, careful not to put too much pressure on his left foot. "Lindsey, I'm not buying what you're saying to me. Maybe I have an overblown ego here, but I can't believe you're just dusting me off. Not after everything we've shared, the way we've obviously come to feel about each other.''

''Well…''

''Talk to me,'' he said. ''Please. What's really going on with you? What is the secret you're keeping from me? Don't you trust me enough by now to tell me the truth?

''Ah, hell, Lindsey, I love you, don't you realize that? I am very much in love with you, Lindsey Patterson. I want to marry you, make babies with you, spend the rest of my life with you. I love you more than I can even tell you, I swear to God I do.''

Lindsey burst into tears. ''You do not. Don't say that to me, Cable Montana. Don't you dare say that you're in love with me.'' She dashed tears from her cheeks. ''I'd like you to leave now. Please.''

''No,'' Cable said, leaning back against the sofa cushions again. ''Not until you tell me why you're crying.''

''I'm crying because…because I'm a romantic at heart and it's very sad that this moment won't have a happy-ever-after ending. I'm very honored to think that you love me, that you're asking me to…to marry you, be your wife and…but you see, Cable, I just…I just don't…love you.''

Lindsey pressed her lips tightly together to stifle a sob that threatened to escape when she saw the hurt, the pain, that swept over Cable's face, then settled in the depths of his beautiful and expressive green eyes.

Cable took a sharp breath, then pushed himself to his feet, teetering slightly as he caught the majority of his weight on his right foot.

"Well," he said, his voice sounding strange and gritty to his own ears, "that's clear enough. I love you, but you don't love me. I guess there's nothing more to say on the subject."

"I...no, there isn't," Lindsey whispered.

Cable limped to the front door, opened it, then turned to look at Lindsey again.

"I hope you'll be very happy, Lindsey," he said quietly, "but, ah, damn it, I wish..." He shook his head as emotions choked off his words, then left the house, closing the door with a soft click.

Lindsey wrapped her hands around her elbows and rocked jerkily in the chair as the devastatingly painful chill of emptiness, loneliness and heartbreak swept through her. Tears streamed down her face.

"I love you so much, Cable," she said, crying openly. "I'm so sorry I hurt you, so very sorry. Oh, God, Cable, I love you, I love you, I..."

Lindsey covered her face with her hands and wept.

## Chapter Thirteen

The whole town was buzzing.

During the next three days, even those who usually didn't take part in gossipy bulletins were eager to hear if the breakup between Lindsey Patterson and Sheriff Montana was really true.

Some people sighed with sadness, others speculated as to what had gone awry between the wonderful couple, but no one approached either Lindsey or Cable on the subject. The original goal of the charade was working—the heartbroken love-birds were left alone.

The mum's-the-word philosophy, however, did not include Aunt Charity.

On the evening of the third day since the heart-wrenching scene in Lindsey's living room, Cable received a message from the dispatcher at the office that Aunt Charity wished to see him in her apartment at Hamilton House.

Cable was getting ready to go off duty and radioed back that he'd stop by the hotel on his way home and to please call Aunt Charity and tell her he was on his way.

In the apartment on the top floor of Hamilton House, Cable kissed each of the aunts on the cheek, then settled onto the sofa.

"I got your message, Aunt Charity," Cable said after declining Aunt Prudence's offer of a cup of tea. "I'm here. How are you feeling?"

"I'm mad as a wet hen," Aunt Charity said, narrowing her eyes.

"Because you have to rest so much?" Cable said. "You know that Ben has your best interests at heart. You'd better be following his directions to the letter." He paused. "Do as I say, not as I do. I'm not supposed to be driving my Land Rover with this bum ankle but..." He shrugged.

"I'm not spitting nails because I'm bored with sitting here," Aunt Charity said. "I'm torqued to the max at you and Lindsey."

Cable sighed and eased his throbbing left ankle onto his right knee.

"Yeah, well, I can't help you out there," he said. "It's over, done, finished. I love Lindsey, but she doesn't love me."

"Bull—" Aunt Charity started, then glanced quickly at Prudence "—stuff. That girl is in love with you, Cable Montana, and it's as clear as the nose on my face. I can't believe that you're giving up so easily. Where's your fighting spirit, big boy? Why are you rolling over and playing dead?"

"Aunt Charity," Cable said wearily, "there's nothing wrong with my hearing. Lindsey told me in no uncertain terms that she is not in love with me."

"And you believe that malarkey?" Aunt Charity said, none too quietly.

"Don't excite yourself, Charity," Aunt Prudence said. "You'll just tire yourself out and have to go to bed earlier than usual. Do calm down. I know that our Lindsey is in love with our Cable, too, but I'm not raising my voice on the subject."

Cable frowned. "You both honestly believe that Lindsey really does love me, but won't admit it for heaven only knows what reason?"

"Oh, my stars, yes," Aunt Prudence said. "One only has to look into Lindsey's eyes to see the love shining there for you, Cable dear."

"Damn straight," Aunt Charity said, nodding.

"Charity, please do refrain from using profanities in our home," Prudence said. "It does upset my sensibilities so when you speak those words."

"I'm sorry, Pru," Charity said, "but I'm just at my wit's end with Lindsey and this hotshot here."

"Now wait," Cable said, raising one hand. "Suppose, just suppose, that you're right. Suppose Lindsey really does love me. Why wouldn't she tell me when I told her how I felt about her? Then again, all along I've felt there was something she was keeping from me—a secret of some kind—that she just didn't trust me quite enough to reveal.

"What if…" Cable stared into space. "What if that secret of hers is what is keeping her from admitting that she loves me? I mean, hell—excuse me, Aunt Prudence—there's nothing in this world that we couldn't handle together if we loved each other."

"Now you're cookin', good-lookin'," Aunt Charity said, beaming. "Are you stepping up to the plate again in this ball game? Your entire future happiness—yours and Lindsey's—is hanging in the balance here."

"You're right," Cable said slowly. "Yeah, you're absolutely on the money. I gave up too easily. I went down for the count without putting up a respectable fight for the woman I love. I've been dragging around feeling sorry for myself instead of taking action. Even Buddy has been behaving like the angel he really isn't because I've been such a gloomy grump.''

Cable settled his Stetson firmly on his head, then lowered his left foot carefully to the floor. He stood, then crossed the room to kiss each of the aunts.

''Thank you, ladies,'' he said, ''for making me come out of the ether. Stay tuned. Good night.''

Cable left the apartment and the aunts exchanged matching smiles.

''Now that's more like it,'' Charity said.

''Yes, Charity,'' Prudence said, ''it certainly is.''

At noon the next day Cable limped into The Green Thumb, which to his approval was bustling with customers. All eyes turned to watch him as he approached Lindsey where she was bent over a bush in a bucket.

''Lindsey,'' he said.

Lindsey straightened and spun around so fast she teetered on her feet.

''Cable?'' she said, her eyes wide. ''What—''

Cable shoved a bouquet of long-stemmed red roses at her, forcing her to take the green-tissue-wrapped flowers. He stepped close to her, framed her face gently in his hands and kissed her deeply.

''I love you, Lindsey Patterson,'' he said, when he finally released her.

With that Cable turned and hobbled out of the nursery, leaving behind a stunned Lindsey and an excited bunch of onlookers, who were already contemplating who to relate the marvelously romantic scene to first.

Lindsey blinked, placed one hand on her racing heart, then closed her eyes as she inhaled the lovely aroma of the gorgeous roses. In the next instant she frowned and stared into space.

Had that whole scene really taken place? she thought. Well, yes, it had, because she was holding the flowers that were proof of it, plus she could still feel Cable's passionate kiss.

But why had Cable marched in there, given her flowers and kissed the socks off her? It didn't make sense, not one little bit. He knew it was over between them, because she'd told him—well, lied to him—that she just didn't love him as he loved her.

What was he up to? What was going on in that complicated male mind of his?

Glenna-Sue came rushing to where Lindsey stood, the older woman carrying a vase half-filled with water.

''Oh, such beautiful roses,'' Glenna-Sue gushed. ''The flower of sweethearts. It's enough to bring tears to my eyes. And the way Sheriff Montana kissed you? Oh, now I really am going to cry. Aren't you thrilled with what just happened, Lindsey?''

"No, I am not," Lindsey said, narrowing her eyes. "I can't be thrilled about something I don't understand. It's over between me and Cable, Glenna-Sue. He knows that and I know that."

"I think he forgot," Glenna-Sue said, beaming. "Would you like to put the roses in this vase so they'll stay fresh and pretty?"

"Fine, then you take them home, because I don't intend to. I don't need a reminder in my house that Cable has lost his mind."

"What Cable has lost, I do believe," Glenna-Sue said, "is his heart…forever."

The next day after closing The Green Thumb, Lindsey drove home with visions in her exhausted mind of a bubble bath and an early-to-bed evening.

She had not slept well the previous night. The confusion over Cable's arrival at the nursery with the roses, combined with the chilling ache in her heart from missing him, had caused her to toss and turn through long, lonely hours of the dark, dreary night.

When she drove onto her street, her eyes widened as she saw Cable's Land Rover parked in her driveway and the man in question standing on her front porch.

She parked next to Cable's vehicle, leaving him room to back out, something he was going to do, she fumed, within the next sixty seconds.

Lindsey marched across the yard and planted her hands on her hips when she stopped in front of Cable.

"What are you doing on my front porch, Cable Montana?" she said.

"Waiting for you to arrive," he said, smiling pleasantly. "I brought you a tuna-fish casserole for your dinner, Lindsey. I made it myself from scratch, which indicates I'm not a total washout in the kitchen. I'm not sure you're aware of that, but now you know. It's important that you know that about me, you know what I mean? Well, enjoy your dinner. See ya." He pushed the towel-covered dish at Lindsey, then touched one fingertip to the brim of his Stetson.

As Cable started toward the Land Rover, Lindsey stared at the bundle in her hands, then shook her head slightly.

"Wait a minute," she yelled, spinning around. "Why did you bring me my dinner? Not that tuna-fish casserole qualifies for that title. Are there peas in this thing? Forget that. And why did you bring me roses and what in the blue blazes are you up to?''

"Can't talk now," Cable said, opening the door to the Land Rover. "I've got a call coming in over the radio. Oh, the wire barriers in front of the bushes in my backyard are cemented into place now. I thought you'd like to be kept up-to-date on that. Buddy seems to have turned the corner on his rotten behavior and is being as good as gold. Great, huh? Our boy is really shaping up. Bye.''

"*Our* boy?'' Lindsey said incredulously, as Cable drove away. "*Our* boy's father has slipped over the edge of his sanity, that's what, and I have a dreadful feeling that I'm not far behind him.''

The next morning, when Lindsey opened the front door to her house to get the newspaper, there was a foil-wrapped package on the porch with a note taped to it. She glanced quickly around, snatched up the parcel and took it inside, closing the door behind her. She tore off the note with a trembling hand and read it aloud.

"These are hot-from-the-oven cinnamon rolls from Hamilton House to go with your morning coffee. Sweets for the sweet. I hope you have a wonderful day, my Lindsey. Love, Cable.''

Sudden tears filled Lindsey's eyes and she hugged the gift tightly, vaguely aware that she was probably smushing the delicious rolls into a gooey mess.

"Oh, this is so sweet, so thoughtful, so..." She sniffled, then drew a steadying breath. "So completely nuts. What's wrong with that man? Didn't he understand a word I said? Why is he doing these romantic, wonderful things?"

Lindsey did not sleep well again that night. She had a dream in which Cable had the starring role. He was holding an enormous bouquet of roses that turned into a balancing act of casserole dishes, then shifted to him standing next to a tower of cinnamon rolls.

And through it all he was smiling...a warm, loving smile that caused Lindsey to awaken and stare into the darkness, missing Cable with an aching intensity that was beyond anything she had ever known.

She loved him so much and it was very obvious that he sincerely loved her, she thought, pulling the sheet to beneath her chin. He was, apparently, taking a page from the matchmakers' handbook, attempting to wear her down and get her to admit that she loved him as much as he loved her.

And she did. Oh, yes, she truly did.

But that didn't change the cold truth, that there was no hope for a future with Cable. Not now. Not ever.

The whole town probably knew that Sheriff Montana was on a mission to recapture her heart. The people were no doubt cheering him on, waiting with wistful sighs to hear all about the happy ending between the lovebirds.

But that wasn't going to happen, Lindsey thought miserably. This wasn't a romance novel, this was reality in its crummiest form. Cable had to leave her alone, because it was just too painful for her to bear.

Lindsey rolled over onto her stomach, buried her face in her pillow and cried.

The next day Cable delivered a plate of burned-to-a-crisp coconut fig cookies to the nursery, kissed Lindsey until she couldn't breathe, then turned and limped away, not having spoken a word.

The day after that Lindsey found a fluffy gray kitten in a wicker basket on her front porch with a note from Cable suggesting that her new pet and Buddy have a play date soon so they could get to know each other. Lindsey adored the kitten at first sight and named her Rose.

The following day there was no sign of Cable,

nor were there any surprises waiting for Lindsey at the nursery or at her house.

She found herself waiting, watching, then finally admitted as she prepared for bed that night that she felt rather disappointed from Cable's absence and lack of attention.

"See, Rose?" she said to the kitten, who curled up next to her on the bed. "I'm certifiably insane. I wanted Cable to leave me alone. Now he is, and here I am pouting. When they come to take me to the funny farm, I'll demand that you get to go along. Okay?"

The kitten purred and Lindsey cried again, for all that might have been but would never be.

After work the next day Lindsey's heart soared when she turned onto her street and saw Cable's Land Rover in her driveway. In the next instant she told herself to get a grip, that she did not want him there and this time, by gum, she was going to, somehow, get that message across loud and very, very clear.

"What!" she said to Cable, when she stood in front of him on her porch.

Do not, she ordered herself, look at this man's broad shoulders in that black western shirt, and those long, muscular legs being hugged by faded jeans. Do not dwell on the fact that his green eyes were enough to die for, and those lips of his were ecstasy waiting to happen. Do not think about how very, very much in love with him you are, and always will be.

"I brought a toy for your kitten," he said, smiling. "I heard you named her Rose. That's nice. It means you really liked the roses I brought you that day. Anyway, I wanted to give this toy to Rose myself so she can get to know me."

"That's it," Lindsey said. "I've had it. This is the last straw. Come inside, Cable, because we're going to have a serious discussion."

Cable glanced heavenward in a silent plea, then followed Lindsey into her house.

In the living room, Lindsey waved one hand to indicate that Cable should sit on the sofa. She walked in front of him, then stopped abruptly with her back to him. She could literally feel the heat of Cable's gaze, but knew she had to gather her courage and strength before she could speak to him.

This wasn't fair, she thought miserably. She'd already gotten through, somehow, the heartbreaking scene of telling Cable—lying to Cable—about the fact that she simply didn't love him as he loved her. Now she had to do it all again and it was ripping her to shreds. How dare he make her suffer such agony a second time?

Lindsey mentally snatched up the anger as it coursed through her and hung on to it for dear life. She spun around and planted her hands on her hips.

"I'm furious with you, Cable Montana," she said, hoping her voice was steadier than it sounded to her own ears. "You've changed the rules we set up for the charade without consulting me.

"Why? Why are you doing these crazy things? Bringing me flowers. A gruesome tuna-fish casserole that even had peas in it. Cookies as hard as hockey pucks. A kitten—no, I won't rant and rave about Rose because I adore her, but it was sweet and romantic of you to give her to me and—

"Why? Why are you being sweet and romantic? Why aren't you following the game plan we set up? It was working out perfectly, just as we planned. It was over between us and the matchmakers were leaving us alone. Now? Good heavens, Cable, you seem to have joined the rank and file of the matchmakers yourself."

Cable nodded slowly and ran one hand over his chin in a gesture that was so familiar, so him, that Lindsey had to draw a quick breath to swallow the sob that caught in her throat.

"Yes, I did change the rules," Cable said quietly, "but I had to because I'm not the same man I was when the charade began. I am deeply and forever in love with you, Ms. Lindsey Patterson."

"Don't go there, Cable," Lindsey said wearily, sinking onto an easy chair. "Please, just don't. We've been through this and there's nothing more to be said on the subject. I'm asking you to please stop giving me flowers and tuna fish. It's not going to accomplish anything except keeping things stirred up with the people in town and I really can't handle it anymore."

Cable narrowed his eyes and there was an edge to his voice when he spoke. "Well, I can't handle what is going on anymore, either, Lindsey. You are *still* keeping something from me that is standing between us like a brick wall.

"I'm a desperate man who is fighting for his life. Does that sound overly dramatic? Well, it isn't because *you* are my life, my future happiness, and I'll make lousy cookies and bring you ten kittens, and do whatever I have to to get you to trust me enough to tell me what you're hiding from me. Trust me enough to admit that you love me every bit as much as I love you."

Lindsey shook her head. "No, I—"

"Damn it, Lindsey," Cable yelled, "don't do this to us. Say the words. Tell me you love me."

Lindsey jumped to her feet, tears filling her eyes and spilling onto her pale cheeks.

"All right," she said, matching Cable's volume. "I love you. Okay? I love you with every breath in my body. Okay? I love you, Cable—'' a sob escaped from her lips ''—more than I can ever begin to tell you in words. Okay, Cable, are you satisfied now? You did it. You stole my heart and I don't know how to get it back.''

''Oh, thank God,'' Cable said, closing his eyes for a long moment, then looking at Lindsey again. ''This is wonderful, so fantastic I—''

''No, it's not!'' Lindsey shrieked. ''It's the most devastating thing that has ever happened to me. I'm in love with a man who is in love with me, and nothing is going to come of it except an endless stretch of emptiness and loneliness and…oh, Cable, please, just go, leave me alone. I'm falling apart here, and I'm terrified that I won't know how to put the pieces that are me back together again. Go. Just go. Please.''

Cable got to his feet, wincing as he put too much pressure on his injured ankle. He closed the distance between him and Lindsey and gripped her shoulders. She sniffled and stared at one of the pearly snaps in the middle of his shirt.

''Look at me,'' he said gently.

''No.''

''Look…at…me.''

Lindsey sighed and raised her head to meet Cable's gaze, her eyes glistening with tears.

''I don't understand this at all,'' he said. ''My

God, Lindsey, you're in love with me and I love you and…the future is ours to share, don't you see? I want to marry you and—''

''And what?'' Lindsey interrupted. ''Make beautiful babies with me? That's important to you, isn't it, Cable? Being a father, creating a child with the woman you love? That's part of the pretty picture you paint in your mind when you envision us being together as husband and wife. Isn't it?''

''Well, yeah, sure,'' he said, obviously confused. ''We'd be a family—you, me, our children. Oh, and Buddy and Rose and…what's wrong with that picture you say I've painted in my mind? I'm definitely not getting what's upsetting you.'' He narrowed his eyes. ''It's your secret. Right? This all has something to do with what you won't tell me, the truth about…damn it, Lindsey, about what?''

Fresh tears filled Lindsey's eyes and a chilling shudder swept through her.

''The babies, Cable,'' Lindsey said, sobbing openly. ''I…I can never give you a child. I'm not able to have children.''

''What?'' Cable said, frowning.

''I told you that my mother and father had me late in life,'' Lindsey rushed on. ''My mother had a rare medical condition that caused her own body to destroy her eggs. By some miracle, I guess, there was one little egg that survived and…and here I am…and…I inherited that strange and horrible condition, Cable, and I've had a multitude of tests run. There will be no miracle for me. Not ever. I'm barren. There are no eggs, there is no chance of me ever having a baby.''

''But—''

''No!'' Lindsey stepped backward, forcing Cable to release his hold on her. ''Don't say anything, Cable, because I heard it all three years ago, before I moved here. I was in love with a man named Dennis, and we'd had a relationship for over a year. We began to talk about the future, about getting married and…''

She drew a shuddering breath.

''I believed in Dennis, in the strength of our love, in what we had together. I…I told him I couldn't have children and he…he…''

''He what?'' Cable asked, his heart pounding.

''Dennis became angry, said I'd deceived him, had passed myself off as a…a complete woman when I really wasn't. No man, he said, would marry a woman who couldn't give him a child. He walked out of my life, but before he left he shook his head and said his anger was gone and all he felt for me was pity.''

Cable swore under his breath.

''I knew then,'' Lindsey went on, a sob catching

in her throat, "that I would never allow myself to fall in love again, would never marry. And I would keep my secret because I couldn't bear the pity, the anger, directed toward me. Not again.

"Oh, sure, you could stand here right now and tell me it doesn't matter that I can't give you a baby, but in time it would chip away at our love, destroy what we had. You'd come to resent me and my inadequacy. You're a normal, healthy man, and you deserve to have a child. I can't give you one, Cable. I can't.

"Now do you understand?" she said, dashing tears from her cheeks. "We have no future together, despite what we might feel for each other. You'll forget me in time. You'll find a woman, a complete woman, who can give you all the babies you want. Oh, please, please, go and leave me alone, Cable."

Cable took a deep breath and let it out slowly, puffing his cheeks.

"That's it?" he said. "That's your deep, dark secret? That's what you gave enough power to to erect a wall between us? The fact that you can't have children?"

Lindsey nodded as she struggled and failed to stop the flow of tears that streamed down her face.

"Well," Cable said, "I sure know what I need to do now that I know the long-awaited truth."

"So do I," Lindsey said, sniffling again. "You need to walk out that door and never come back. You need to stop baking the worst cookies ever to come out of an oven. You need to erase the existence of tuna fish from your memory bank. You need to…" She stopped speaking as tears choked off her words.

"No, no, forget that ridiculous list you just rattled off." A smile began to form on Cable's lips and widened into a full-blown grin. "What I need to do is contact one of the architect extraordinaire MacAllisters and have plans for a huge house drawn up to our specifications. We're going to need a lot of room for all our kids and pets."

"Did that bump on your head you suffered when you rescued Joey affect your hearing?" Lindsey said. "We are not getting married. There will be no humongous house. There will be no children for us to love and nurture. Are you getting this yet, Cable?"

"Lindsey," he said, framing her face in his hands, "if I wasn't so happy about knowing you love me as much as I love you, I'd be really ticked. Do you honestly believe that I'd be marrying you for your ability to reproduce? That blows my mind. You're selling me so short it's a crime I should arrest you for."

"But—"

"But nothing," Cable said firmly. "I won't come to resent you in the years ahead, my beautiful dope. I will love you in the years ahead for who you are. My Lindsey. My wife. My soul mate. My life. I will love you and the slew of kids we're going to adopt."

"You'd be…be willing to adopt babies?" Lindsey said, hardly above a whisper. "Do you truly mean that? They wouldn't be children of your body, Cable."

"They would be children of my heart, Lindsey, and that's what counts in the long run. My heart, your heart, entwined, will make those children ours."

"Oh, Cable, I don't know what to say. I—"

"Say yes," he said. "Say that you'll marry me, be my wife, the mother of the children who are waiting for us somewhere in this world so we can bring them home. Say yes, Lindsey, please."

"I…" Lindsey flung her arms around Cable's neck and he wrapped his arms tightly around her. "Yes! I never allowed myself to daydream that there might be a man who would be willing to adopt because I was convinced I was just setting myself up to have my heart broken again. Oh, Cable, I love you so much. We really can have it all…together."

"No doubt about it," he said, smiling. "We'll

build that big house and…ow! Rose is crawling up my leg and she has very sharp little nails.'' He released his hold on Lindsey and pried the kitten off his leg to hold her at eye level. ''Hello, where were you hiding?''

''She naps a lot,'' Lindsey said, ''because she's, well, she's a baby. Now she wants to be the center of attention. She's so cute. Smart, too.''

''Of course,'' Cable said. ''I picked her out. She's a Montana. And you're going to be a Montana, Ms. Patterson, and the sound of that…Lindsey Montana…is music to my ears. Ah, Lindsey, I love you so much. I came so close to losing you and—no, forget that. It's all behind us now. The future is ours.''

''Yes, Cable, it is, and I love you beyond measure,'' Lindsey said, her eyes brimming with happy tears this time.

''Hey, Rose,'' Cable said, ''you'd better take as many naps as you can, little girl, because there's another Montana in this family who is going to want to play until the two of you drop.''

Rose meowed.

''Buddy,'' Lindsey and Cable said in unison, then burst into laughter.

Their laughter filled the room to overflowing, chasing away the pain and loneliness of the days and nights Lindsey and Cable had just endured, and the dark secret that had held Lindsey in an iron fist for so many, many years.

The future was theirs. It belonged to Cable and Lindsey, Rose and Buddy, and all the Montanas yet to come.

The future was theirs...forever.

\*     \*     \*     \*     \*

*Look for bestselling author*
*Joan Elliott Pickart's next*
*Special Edition novel*
*in Summer 2001!*

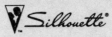

# SPECIAL EDITION™

## Save $1.00 off your purchase of any Silhouette Special Edition® title

Experience it all with Silhouette Special Edition®—
Life, love and family!

Pick up a Special Edition® novel for an emotional,
compelling story that captures the intensity of living,
loving and creating a family in today's world.

---

## $1.00 OFF!
your purchase of any
Silhouette Special Edition® title

RETAILER: Harlequin Enterprises Ltd. will pay the face value of this coupon plus 8¢ if
submitted by customer for this specified product only. Any other use constitutes fraud.
Coupon is non-assignable. Void if taxed, prohibited or restricted by law. Consumer must
pay any government taxes. Valid in U.S. only. For reimbursement submit coupons and proof
of sales directly to: Harlequin Enterprises Ltd., P.O. Box 880478, El Paso, TX 88588-0478,
U.S.A. Cash value 1/100¢.

**107344**

Coupon expires July 31, 2001.
Valid at retail outlets in U.S. only.

5 65373 00076 2    (8100) 0 10734

---

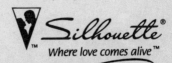

Silhouette®
*Where love comes alive*™

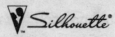

# SPECIAL EDITION™

## Save $1.00 off your purchase of any Silhouette Special Edition® title

Experience it all with Silhouette Special Edition®—
Life, love and family!

Pick up a Special Edition® novel for an emotional,
compelling story that captures the intensity of living,
loving and creating a family in today's world.

---

# $1.00 OFF!
your purchase of any
Silhouette Special Edition® title

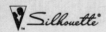

```
5 2 6 0 2 7 0 8
```

---

Where love comes alive™

Coming soon from

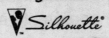 Silhouette®

# SPECIAL EDITION™

An exciting new miniseries
from bestselling author

# SUSAN MALLERY

LONE STAR CANYON

In the small town of
Lone Star Canyon, Texas,
the men are what fantasies
are made of—impossibly
handsome and rugged—
and the women are tempting
enough to melt their hearts.

Come visit Lone Star Canyon—where romance
and passion are as hot as the Texas sun!

**THE RANCHER NEXT DOOR**
(SE #1358, on sale November 2000)

**UNEXPECTEDLY EXPECTING!**
(SE #1370, on sale January 2001)

**WIFE IN DISGUISE**
(SE #1383 on sale March 2001)

*Available at your favorite retail outlet.*

 Silhouette®

*Where love comes alive*™

Visit Silhouette at www.eHarlequin.com     SSELSC

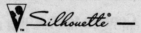

If you enjoyed what you just read,
then we've got an offer you can't resist!

# Take 2 bestselling love stories FREE!
# Plus get a FREE surprise gift!

Clip this page and mail it to Silhouette Reader Service™

| IN U.S.A. | IN CANADA |
|---|---|
| 3010 Walden Ave. | P.O. Box 609 |
| P.O. Box 1867 | Fort Erie, Ontario |
| Buffalo, N.Y. 14240-1867 | L2A 5X3 |

**YES!** Please send me 2 free Silhouette Special Edition® novels and my free surprise gift. Then send me 6 brand-new novels every month, which I will receive months before they're available in stores. In the U.S.A., bill me at the bargain price of $3.80 plus 25¢ delivery per book and applicable sales tax, if any*. In Canada, bill me at the bargain price of $4.21 plus 25¢ delivery per book and applicable taxes**. That's the complete price and a savings of at least 10% off the cover prices—what a great deal! I understand that accepting the 2 free books and gift places me under no obligation ever to buy any books. I can always return a shipment and cancel at any time. Even if I never buy another book from Silhouette, the 2 free books and gift are mine to keep forever. So why not take us up on our invitation. You'll be glad you did!

235 SEN C224
335 SEN C225

| Name | (PLEASE PRINT) | |
|---|---|---|
| Address | Apt.# | |
| City | State/Prov. | Zip/Postal Code |

\* Terms and prices subject to change without notice. Sales tax applicable in N.Y.
\*\* Canadian residents will be charged applicable provincial taxes and GST.
  All orders subject to approval. Offer limited to one per household.
® are registered trademarks of Harlequin Enterprises Limited.

SPED00                                    ©1998 Harlequin Enterprises Limited

# COMING NEXT MONTH

### #1381 HER UNFORGETTABLE FIANCÉ—Allison Leigh
*Stockwells of Texas*

To locate her missing mother, Kate Stockwell teamed up
with private investigator Brett Larson to masquerade as a married
couple. Together they discovered that desire still burned between
them. But when former fiancé Brett asked Kate to be his wife for
real, she feared that she could never provide all that he wanted...

### #1382 A LOVE BEYOND WORDS—Sherryl Woods

Firefighter Enrique Wilder saved Allie Matthews from the rubble
of her home and forever changed her silent world. A shared
house and an undeniable chemistry caused passion to run high.
But would Allie be able to love a man who lived so close to
danger?

### #1383 WIFE IN DISGUISE—Susan Mallery
*Lone Star Canyon*

Josie Scott decided it was time to resolve the past and showed
up at her ex-husband's door a changed woman. Friendship and
closure were all that Josie was after, until she looked into
Del Scott's eyes. Finally, with a chance to explore their
daunting past, would the two discover that love was still alive?

### #1384 STANDING BEAR'S SURRENDER—Peggy Webb

Forlorn former Blue Angel pilot Jim Standing Bear had lost his
ambition...until he found gentle beauty Sarah Sloan. She
reminded Jim that he was all man. But Sarah—committed to
caring for another—would have to choose between loyalty and
true love....

### #1385 SEPARATE BEDROOMS...?—Carole Halston

All Cara LaCroix wanted was to fulfill her grandmother's final
wish—to see her granddaughter marry a good man. So when
childhood friend Neil Griffen offered his help, Cara accepted.
Could their brief marriage of convenience turn into an everlasting
covenant of love?

### #1386 HOME AT LAST—Laurie Campbell

Desperate for a detective's help, Kirsten Laurence called old
flame J. D. Ryder. She didn't have romance on her mind, but they
soon found themselves in each other's arms. Would their embrace
withstand the shocking revelation of Kirsten's long-kept secret?